The

The Cherry Orchard

JONATHAN LOVEJOY

Armageddon Publishing
All rights reserved.

Cover: *Head of a Young Girl*, 1890
William Adolphe Bouguereau (1825-1905)

ISBN-10: 0692316590
ISBN-13: 978-0692316597

For every Sarah

For it is a shame even to speak of those things

Which are done of them in secret...

Ephesians 5:12

Austria

This is a lawn of devastating beauty. The place where I find myself so much of the day—often because my husband is away, I think. What good is it to be a billionaire's wife, except to swim in the Ocean of Prosperity—where money is never spent so much as it is *sent*—in exchange for whatever it is I want under the sun. Forty two acres and a broom in the kitchen, touched by no maid except the Hands of Mine (my hands), when the phantom dust collects on or about the white tile floor.

Far from where I have swept the kitchen, I walk the lawn of dreams, the backyard of this fabulous white mansion home. Three weeks out of every month, my Petroleum Pete is gone, flying and dying every day around the world with others who fly and die with him—worried about gas prices and car prices and loving what small prices there are to pay for their successes, mainly in the stifling of any real sense of morality, and the measured abandonment of their longsuffering wives, and the treasured abandonment of their children.

What children I've had to deal with, thankfully, don't really belong to me at all, but borrowed from the womb of a previous marriage—five, yes, five brats I raised heartily—then hurried them the Hell away from this property to their own Ivy League lives—where they all hide and wait for time to bring them along. They are not mine—I could care less, really, having been lucky enough not to have had my insides split open by his corrupted seed grown inside of me. I gave birth to none of them, and his three daughters I despise even more than his two sons.

School and graduate school—school and graduate school, if I hear it one more time I'll swirl and stroke and die.

Spoiled, rich bastards are his two sons. Peter Jr. and Paul, Paulie and Peter, Peter and Paul, Paulie and Pete... sounds like a damned mobster movie. They both bore me and sicken me to no end. They were too old for me to properly train when I married their father; they were little lords of the manor when he was around and when he wasn't, because whatever I did to them they told their absentee father upon his many returns and I grew tired of his eternal punishments and restrictions. Oh yes. In the homes of the rich, behind the closed palace doors, there be greater sins than grieves the heart of man—for what the poor and the dispossessed know of is magnified a hundred fold among the rich and the privileged. What motivations there are among us are the same as everyone else, however mysterious, unavoidable, or unidentifiable they may be. What motivations were there for me, as I burned my three daughters red, black and blue with corporal punishment for every small infraction from the casual breaking of a dish to the uncasual slipping of a grade, for eyes wide open when they should be closed in sleep, to dinners not properly eaten—the spankings, whippings, canings and the occasional fisting (the punching kind) were carefully controlled, bound up and channeled in the name of discipline, from when they were three, five and eight years old until they all conveniently left home for college—my oldest ("daughter" if you will) being made to understand just this last Thanksgiving that I will never be disrespected by her, as the bruises I pinched onto her sides attested. I made her pull her dress down and hold it at her waist—a twenty two year old grad student—and in my bathroom I pinched her sides until I saw the tears run down her eyes like tiny streams of contrition and disillusionment. She made no sound, but the tears ran steady. And while she cried, for the first time I made her kiss me smack on the mouth; oh, yes… I did. *If you're goin' to therapy for this then goddammit lets give 'em something to listen to you bitch about...* what is the psycho-sexual motivation that causes a mother to make a fifteen year old girl pull her jeans down and her bra up, and "wail the tar" (as my Momma used to say) out of her little fat ass until she would need medical attention if I went any farther? What is this motivation? Is it the hatred I have always felt inside for their abusive, absentee father? Mr. Rich Son of a Bitch he is, and that right true, you can believe, being the son of the bitchiest bitch since the wicked witch herself. Is it boredom that causes me to make a twelve year old girl raise her shirt up, while I twist her little undeveloped nipples hard enough to make her scream deeper than she ever has, then sink into a depression she will never fully recover from as a grown woman? Is it the old fashioned, run of the mill sexual frustration that caused me to get behind an eighteen year old prom queen and put my hands under her t-shirt and twist her breasts until she slobbered onto the bathroom counter from the pain?

At their graduations from public, not private school, I watched all three of their distinct little personalities tempered by the same thread—the one that runs through my bloodline to contaminate theirs with pain and sorrow. I was unproud as they walked in dignity to accept a diploma from the State of Connecticut. Unimpressed by each of them as they made it through the first stage of this tired life. I was unmoved by the memories of blood, pain and tears, and the voice of their father saying *"you can do what you want to these girls. As a matter of fact, however much pain it takes I want you to make young ladies out of all three of 'em.* Unapologetic as I remember the way my breasts tingled when I first removed my own bra to administer a double paddling to Kym and Penelope, my two oldest—even while they snickered in braces with their hands bound up behind their backs standing there nude. Was it nervousness that made them snicker at their stepmother's exposed, swinging breasts? Did my girls laugh because my breasts hang low and natural and are too big and floppy for my frame? What motivates a woman to remove her bra and paddle her step daughters to bruising and tears? What do I give a damn for their droopy manner, nearly devoid of smiles, what of their passive aggressive submissiveness and their doormat sensibilities? There are no Paris Hiltons here.

And what of their father? Peter. Peter Nicklaus. "Jack" Bishop, we all know. Oil company executive, only forty six today. Became a billionaire when his energy company (that's all I know about it), Bishop Industries—

was bought by a company that merged with BP. We are worth a measly 1.2 billion dollars. Peter Jack. Jack Nicklaus Bishop. Hardly a month goes by that he is not in Russia or Saudi Arabia or Alaska or Hawaii. One of the energy billionaires. So what? Does he offer to take me with him? Which one of his girlfriends goes with him? Which one of his daughters? Did he fuck his oldest daughter one summer in Fiji? This, I do not know for sure. I never asked Penelope but her need for an abortion that fall in her senior year at Harvard certainly came from somewhere. A white blonde with a small waist and a big ghetto ass is rare and special, I suppose. Was that her daddy's baby?

And so I walk the line of trees on my property. Taking a deep breath in the summer green. This is September summer, when all of Pete's dragons have packed up and gone back to whatever university they came from. I stroll the front lawn now, sheltered by the line of trees—remembering the way they will blossom again in the spring. And while I peer into the brief distance, my suspicion is confirmed that there is a figure on one of the property benches.

Is it a man or a woman? I don't care which, I think. But the closer I get, the more I realize—yes, it is a woman.

I leave the long road behind, the asphalt path of Cherry blossom trees, and stroll over to the figure dressed in blue jeans and a black collar shirt, who is engrossed in whatever her pencil and notebook are trying to deliver to the world.

"Hello, there." Beautiful, jade eyes big and round suddenly gaze at me, as if I were a being made of pure lightning. "I'm sorry. I didn't mean to scare you."

"No, it's my fault," she says, closing her notebook. "I stayed way too long."

"Stay as long as you want. Are you a writer?"

"Well, I guess you can call it that. It's what got me into this neighborhood…"

"Oh, you have a home here?"

"No, no… I shouldn't have let you think that. I've never even been published. I drive through here all the time, hoping the gate is open. I park on the road and literally trespass onto your property. It's so beautiful here. The lawn is so plush and green, the trees—it's all so elegant and simple. I always write best when I'm here. Don't ask me why."

"Sarah Bishop," I say, extending an Angelina Perfume Lotion hand to her, already devastated by the emerald beauty of her eyes and the golden, silken smoothness of her skin.

"Lee Goldman. My real name's Austria, *God help me* that's bad."

Goldman—how appropriate is thy name! The same beauty as thy emerald eyes, full lips and golden yellow skin, a white woman tinted as a pale woman of color! Lee Gold! Lee Golding! Where is thy deserved self esteem!

"Austria Goldman—sounds familiar…"

"You're thinking of Oscar Goldman from the Six Million Dollar Man— everybody does. But… did you say *Sarah Bishop*? As in Peter and Sarah Bishop?"

"Guilty."

Our long handshake takes a sudden, serious turn.

"I'm shaking hands with a billionairess."

What sins and sinister motivations bear a handshake? What is the gentle, late summer breeze that blows? What greetings or admonishments do I hear in the woodland leaves nearby, that may even have arisen to a warning? Is it the pretense of Autumn's arrival hence, less than a fortnight away, that cools the winds in our midst? Or is it the supernatural voice of pleading, the warning touch for us to beware, and flee the wrath to come? There are times when the meeting of two people is as fateful as cool and warm air over a spring prairie, whose coming together is borne from the clouds to the ground, to do nothing but kill, steal and destroy—until the whirlwind of their meeting is past. As I take her lovely hand into both of mine, I decide to embrace the pleasure of her company, and the twinge of pain upon her arrival. As we walk the path of the cherry orchard tree, it is as though I have known her from before the world began, holding the arm of this beautiful woman, whose skin is as golden as the sun; as golden as her name.

An elite ruling class is the lynchpin of society. Without it, society would crumble and eventually fall in the ocean. This... the Ocean of Chaos. And where does this so-called elite come from? Is it the clergy—with their puffed up principles and direct line to a so-called higher power, this higher power being God himself—the Creator of the universe we see? Is it the super rich, and their direct line to endless stores of wealth and finance? Is it the intellectual minority—the super gifted thinkers and creative minds, and their allegiance to vast stores of knowledge and learning? From whence comes forth such wisdom as is required to lead the masses of civilization?

The Fear of the Lord is the beginning of wisdom, I think—among which of us is it found! Who shall love and fear the Lord thy God, that they may rule in righteousness, before the end of the age is come, before the rule of the Antichrist is come! For he will step forward in religious, intellectual and financial power such as the world has never seen, and the world will listen to his glowing speeches, and they will marvel at his shining example, until they have no choice but to bow down to his every whim and desire—until they have to bow down and worship him. There has been no world leader, no ruler, no prince, no king, no president nor dictator with the power he will possess—for that power shall come from Satan himself—to give him dominion as the most elite member of society there has ever been, and the absolute ruler over human Creation. The world is poised and ready for his arrival, having lost its stomach for the clergy, the wealthy, and the academic—and from where this man will come from, the world only believes it knows; with what the Bible alludes to in a haze, where we gaze through a glass darkly, to see the eventual and ultimate sign of His coming.

I am the ruler of the estate where we dwell. Well suited to the million dollar home and property. Well accustomed to what pleasures it has to offer. Able now to dismiss its opulence as mere beauty, its extravagance as simple luxury. Somewhere deep inside, as I stroll through the crystal and white porcelain presentation which is our glass and ivory living room, which makes my guest stop and fold her arms and shake her head in amusement park awe, I realize just how little I have to do with such profound wealth and privilege, and I understand that it comes from God. The White Room, as I call it, ivory white from the drapes to the carpet, with so much white fabric, porcelain and crystal in between, is the portal from the real world into the one where I live, which is the alternate reality from what most can ever conceive in their wildest dreams, let alone achieve.

Come wander with me, my lovely Lee Goldman, from my crystal palace to the kitchen, no less magnificent but decidedly less formal, more kitchen than five families would need. But it is a necessary symbol of the wealth we have—the image of wealth we are called to share with the world. Walk with me, Lee Goldman, through this impossible dream! Here, in the rear of our house, as you gaze at the white columns stretched tall above your head to the roof high above us, know that there is no dream of man this grand, nor wish this big in his soul. But as it is written, *"eye hath not seen, nor ear heard, neither have entered into the heart of man, the things which God hath prepared for them that love Him."* The same applies to Heaven on Earth as well.

I watch this strange and beautiful young women (if thirty two is young, it *is* thirteen years younger than me), noticing her descent into a melancholy calm, a peaceful sadness, where there can be no phony smiles nor pretence. "In the Midst of Paradise," she says.

"What's that?"

"Oh… it's a title from some story I wrote a long time ago. About big trouble in this perfect suburban neighborhood."

"What kind of trouble?"

"The kind that kills."

"What other kind is there?" I say it with the same determined dreariness as she, wondering what dark spirit, what omen was just born into the world.

"Have you been on this property a lot?"

"This was the first time I had the nerve to do it in a while. I was gonna drive to the park when something told me to stop and go for a walk. I came in through the gate and saw the bench was empty like always. It's so far away from the house I'm never afraid to sit down. Why was the gate open anyway?"

"Delivery men. I get tired of buzzing them in all the time. Is that a new story you're working on?"

"Believe it or not, I'm starting my fifth novel."

"Really? That's impressive. Have you been published yet?"

"My first novel was rejected almost 2,000 times."

"Two *thousand*? Is that normal?"

"Normal, I guess, when you're a bad writer. But no matter how hard I try, I just can't push it away. It keeps coming back."

"I'm sure you write just fine, Honey."

"Well, they don't think so. I think I've been rejected by every agent in the country."

"What's your first book about? Unless you don't want to say."

"It's about a grown woman whose being abused by her mother. It's like pure domestic violence, only with a suburban mom in her 50's and her thirty two year old daughter. Maybe it's just not compelling enough for a first novel. I don't know."

"What's it called?"

"*Angels*, I think. I don't really know."

Revelation can descend, like a cool mist on a hot summer's day.

"*Angels*. I don't see anything wrong with that. With that title and your unique first name they'd have to buy it and see where you went with such a powerful story."

"Creatively, I've seriously moved on, but for some reason I keep going back. That's why it has so many rejections... I just can't let it go. It's purely an abuse novel though... I'll bet abuse books are permanent bad luck for an unpublished writer."

"Sweetie, I don't know anything about the publishing business but I do know something about luck. Money talks and bullshit walks."

"What do you mean?"

"It's not *what* you know, it's *who* you know."

"Do you really think you could... I mean... you don't even know me and here I am asking..."

"You don't have to ask, Honey."

She looks at me with a sudden anguish, brow wrinkled, and now a frown she covers with her mouth.

"We play tennis and golf with two editors from two of the biggest publishing houses in the world. One is a woman named Susan Marshall—"

"Susan Marshall? Of The Susan Marshall Agency?"

"That's her... but she doesn't run it anymore. She told me that the 'sea of desperation' nearly drowned her. Her exact words were, "*the level of bullshit these poor authors have to endure from literary agents is a tragedy indeed."* I met her at a benefit dinner where Carrie Fisher gave a speech—I didn't even know Susan was a book editor. But being a billionaire's wife means that any and everybody is always looking to do a favor, always inviting me to this or that—and I know they don't really care about me except that I'm rich—"

"Rich and beautiful."

"What?"

"I didn't want to say anything but... oh, what the Hell, you're a beautiful woman."

"Honey you're just saying that because you're happy. You don't think I'm fat?"

She laughs a little and shakes her head. "Ms. Bishop... the only thing fat on you is what you've been trying to hide under that loose shirt. And let me tell you, real or not they're incredible."

"Oh... they're real alright. Real big. Too big."

She can hardly contain her staring. I'm suddenly tempted to cross my arms and change the subject but I resist. And then she tolls the saving bell for me.

"Well, anyway... before I wake up from this dream, you were saying that you can speak to someone who might actually be able to help me."

"No, I'm not saying that at all. I'm saying I *will* speak to someone who *will* be able to help you. Susan's a senior editor.... if she says a book gets in it gets in. Period."

"But seriously, how do you know she'll like the book—its filled with bad luck. It's almost as if God himself doesn't want it published. Yet, He won't let me quit."

"Like I said, Austria. It's not what you know. And I'm not asking God, I'm asking Sue Marshall. You see, in these social circles, the truth is that you don't refuse favors. Especially for something as simple as getting a novel published. Title: *Angels*. Topic: Mother Daughter violence—let the public decide whether or not it's a good novel."

"Or a bad one."

"Like I said, let the public decide."

"What if it bombs?"

"Then you'll publish another one. And you'll keep publishing until either you hit a home run or you strike out. It's time for some good luck now, Austria. From what you've told me, I think you deserve it."

By now, Austria Goldman's arms are crossed and she is leaning against a column, staring at the autumn cherry trees and the leaves blowing in the wind. Then I see her raise her hand to her face, wiping the tears away.

I am drunk with the aroma of spring words. Words that flow like wine from the belly, to describe the inner workings of Heaven and Earth, and the outer workings of mankind. Words tinted sweet with the taste of freedom—the freedom to enjoy the sound of a beautiful younger woman's quiet crying—or the feel of her body against mine. I am drunk with the aroma of spring words—words that captivate and unharness the soul from winter bondage—from the pain of loneliness, to the despair of want and need. These are the living waters that flow—the trees that grow from the fountains of spring, and the solemn nourishment they provide.

These, the waters of spring, the flow of freedom from one body to the next—from the light skinned, green eyed beauty with no self esteem, to the snow white, short haired brunette with the double platinum breasts, the DP's of legend, that would surely put those of Dolly Parton and Oprah Winfrey to shame. As I stand here in the cool autumn breeze, hugging this beautiful young woman, my breasts ache with a tingling they have only echoed in the past, and my heart beats the rhythm of their awakening.

"It's alright," I say. "Just rest. Rest honey."

What to do! Do I truly take her upstairs to my room, and give her a reason to cry! Or do I take her by the arm and waist, and escort her to the kitchen dining table where we belong—at the big pinewood table with white legs, married to the white chairs nearby? I sit her down at one of them, taking my place oh so appropriately, oh so trustworthily in a chair right beside her. I study her face—big eyes now red from crying—brow wrinkled, mouth burdened by a frown. Though she would never know it, I have imagined my cheek pressed tight to hers many times already.

"It's alright, Austria. Everything's fine from now on."

She laughs a little—"You can call me Lee."

"I can't... *Austria*. You just rest."

She puts her head down in sorrow again, to endure another wave of tears. As if on cue, as if to answer the call of Sappho's mighty horn, I firmly pull her head to my breast, bound up so big and tight under my navy collar shirt. There, they are the unwanted pillows of her wildest waking dream, to activate something so deep within; for when her head touches the pillow, her body is racked with a strange, powerful sobbing that jerks in single, regular twitches strong enough, powerful enough to be called convulsions—this rhythm accompanied, layered by the melody of a crying, dying voice—punctuated by the sound of a single loud, coughing sob. Of what pain this is, I do not know, though I can feel the harmonies born from it. With this Desire of Fulfillment, my breasts ache from such a craving as I have never allowed myself to know before, that courses from my bra to my heart, to the shaky breath in my lungs—that begin to flow upward, over my vocal chords like the wind in a place called Carmen Canyon—because of the operatic chords the wind chimes play.

"Un...unbutton my shirt."

Instantly she raises her head and looks at me through the ugly cry, where her face is twisted from the deepest suffering. I nod my head in un-guilty confirmation, repressed by exhilaration.

"Please. Unbutton my shirt."

My breasts are gigantic. As objectivity requires, being that they are many times larger than what most have ever seen. Since I was a very young teenager, they have been the center of my life, though not in lust for myself, but for every other man, woman, boy and girl I have ever met. I have been ridiculed and worshipped, hit and hit upon, threatened and thrown at for 30 years, until I am weary of the public, as anyone with a deformity is eventually cursed to be. But I am not naive, knowing that not all deformities are ugly, as is a lone sequoia nearby a forest of pines.

Beautiful or ugly—it is for others to decide—but it is a sight for the eyes, and a spark of delight to the soul. This I notice myself when I look into a mirror, which I never do in public, lest I be shamed into a hasty retreat. I am a thoroughbred on display for my billionaire husband, to dazzle other wives into submission, if only because they are in disbelief rather than awe. But some memories linger like the smell of burning wood, like a father who treated me like a stranger when I hit fourteen—a brother who called me 'piggy' for two years, and a mother who said *if you keep eatin' like a pig they'll keep growin'*—and even when my stepdaughters were little and I used to masquerade as a mother type—dragging them along with me to the mall and hearing a group of grown black men mumble and one of them turns and says "*gott...DAMN*" being our Father's name taken noisily in vain. My humiliation that day—a 35 year old rich woman with long brunette hair and an ill advised black pullover polo shirt—up 'til that point I had thought the black had hidden them from Vulgarity's point of view. I have heard his voice play in my head over and over for 10 years— "*god...DAMN—god...DAAAYUM—god...DAMN*"—the feeling being enough to make me put down my fork or pencil or paintbrush and just close my eyes and pray that the memory will be taken away forever. Over the years, gradually I have retreated into myself, until my only company has been the sound of my lonely heels echoing through the house, or from where I walk the concrete path under the cherry orchard trees.

The echoes of this walk have drifted across the lawn unheard, to where this beautiful woman once sat with her pencil in hand, pouring that sorrow she feels onto the paper. This beautiful light skinned woman, with hair not quite as straight and black as mine—staring at me through something that looks like pure bewilderment and disbelief. But in the midst of it all, in the misty haze of bewilderment, I watch the sorrow in her eyes turn to sorrowful anticipation, as her hands move on their own to the buttons of my navy blouse. One by one, she fumbles with them, until the cleavage of ages hath fully appeared—where the white skin contrasts with the huge black lace bra they are in. *Open every button,* I say, and she does this, gathering the strength of nerve she needs to all but take the shirt down off my shoulders. All we can do is lock eyes, neither of us knowing what force of perversion this is, that has her sitting at my kitchen table in the afternoon facing me, staring at a black lace bra holding the two biggest breasts she has ever seen.

"In my heart," she says, touching her chest through her gray sweater, taking a deep breath—"in my heart, I thought that *I* had big breasts... because I was a D. I was a D alright. <u>De</u>- *luded*."

For the first time in my life, my breasts are a source of pride. Somewhere beyond contentment and relief, where Modesty can have no life nor purpose to live."I don't know what to do," she says, teary eyed, shaking her head at the edge of delight, but where Sorrow *still* has its life and greater purpose to live. As though to answer the new calling I feel—to pass down what burning I never even knew before (or did I?)—I reach inside the 36J of my left breast and pull it out of my bra, as massive and exposed as the face of the Autumn Moon. She slides out of her kitchen chair to her knees. In the palm of her hand, she lifts it up, staring at the flattened, partially inverted nipple.

What is the innocence of perversion! It is but a single thing, as them who pervertedly nailed our Lord and Savior to the Cross! That this is what he pled God to forgive them for! It is the innocence of perversion, that we don't know what it is that we do!

"Kiss the nipple," I say.

She obeys, so gently—kissing the areola and the nipple, looking up at me the whole time, to see what her punishment for this naïve stupidity will be.

"I swear. I swear to God I've never done this."

"I've never done this either," she says, kissing, blowing gently on the nipple. Watching it grow. The breath of wind makes me shudder. I look down, and we are both staring at once, at the exposed and hardened nipple.

My heartbeat pounds the rhythm of what we do—my breathing sings the melody. I think that for myself—I have denied this part of who I am— that my *breasts* are my sexuality, and that what sex I need to have most likely begins and ends with them. It is the revelation of questions raised— the clarity of the haze I brought into the world so many times, when I took my bra off to paddle my teenage stepdaughters raw.

Austria kisses the raised nipple one last time, before she takes it into her mouth for a full sucking, making me twitch and grab the chair under me with both hands. Then she sucks again, watching my face grimace from the pressure this builds in not just my groin, but in my entire body. She closes her eyes, I suppose to give me privacy, and so she can savor the fountain by where she must have this drink. Austria holds my breasts— beyond the H cup (H for Heavy Hangers), and she begins a steady nursing like a babe on a wet nurse, each suckle pulling it higher, higher up from somewhere deep inside, where lust forms even a cock in a woman's heart to rule or to ride—sucking, pulling me closer toward a haze of dizziness I have not encountered 'til now—then releasing the nipple in a powerful sucking, kissing pull—then I watch her beautiful mouth close around it again, closing my eyes to the pull of renewed energy at my nipple.

These new pulls raise me up to where I feel as though I might float off the chair, and I try not to lose myself—but my voice gets away from me, and I hear it in a moan that sounds like someone is being quietly tortured into a moaning, sobbing cry. This continues for a time I cannot count, and my entire body shakes one mighty time, from the wave of blue fire passing though.

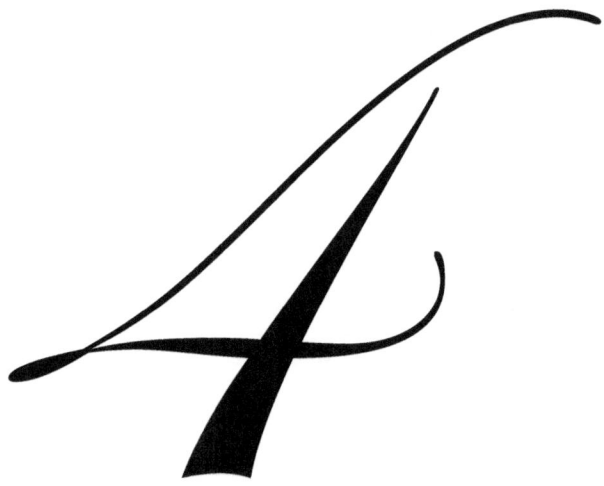

Austria! Thy name is beauty! Our energy is the grandest comfort indeed, solace for lonely unresisting hearts. We sit as though magnetized to one another, me in the cushioned kitchen chair, with the beautiful author in my lap—this woman author whom I have only known within this self-same hour. The gigantic, rounded globe of my breast is still exposed, in pale contrast to the both of hers which are golden. Gray sweater gone, her navy button down shirt (a darker likeness than my own) is unbuttoned just enough, that they are spilled out over the top , both nipples damp from where I was just at with my hands and mouth while she looked on, pulling and shaking and moaning to my twisted heart's content. Inside the both of us, there rages the proverbial storm—the clashing, the coalescence of two individual powers into one.

"Are you a lesbian" is what comes out when I open my mouth—words formed as a cloud of fierce and powerful bewilderment—as the first part to this duet of shameful awareness and fulfillment, to which she answers—

"No."

"Neither am I."

"So what just happened then?"

My answer is to stuff this epic exposure back into its place, my giant bosom, to which she responds so quickly herself in kind.

"Do you want me to go?" she says.

"Now why on Earth would I ever want you to do that?"

"What about your husband? Your family?"

"I don't see how you being my friend has anything to do with my husband. Or my family."

"Is that what we are? Friends?"

Without another word, I lay my head against her cushion breasts, which are now covered in the cloth of midnight blue.

What sins that are common to man, are pervasive along the timeline? Those behind closed doors secrets that cannot be discussed among us—buried so deep as to be invisible when we gather together in public, captured and killed by the spirits of hypocrisy that sustain us? For Austria and I are now aware of this truth, that the spirit of *lesbianism* is universal. It is pervasive among womankind—that those same attributes which light a fire in the belly of man do so as well in the belly of woman—and each woman is particular to her own taste in other women—the lay of the features: the eyes, the nose, the lips—the lay of the breasts: the size, the shape—and the lay of the waist hip ratio: the thinness or thickness of the waist, the narrowness or roundedness of the hips thereof—if they are as straight as a desert highway, or as curved as a mountain forest road. How many women among us have been unfortunate enough to partake of this knowledge—to pull this fruit from that accursed tree?

The Lady Goldman—the Goldman Woman and I sit dumbfounded in the big kitchen, unbeknownst to the silver appliances minding their own business nearby.

"I've always been lucky like this. Strange, otherworldly good luck. And I don't ever remember doing anything to deserve it."

"I believe that luck is simply consequences of the choices we make. I mean… we make our— "

"Make our own luck?" I say. A smile at the mirror in the upper room, as I unbutton my guilty blouse. I know that she gazes in rapt attention. "So you think that good luck comes from good choices?" I say, sliding fully out of the long sleeved navy blouse. In my big, black bra, I study the enormous contrast between the abnormal and the normal—the DisProportionates— the Double Platinum sized boulders and their white cleavage, ruling a body of such average sized normality.

"I'd kill for those."

"I look like a freak," I say, removing the bra fully, to let nature fall where it may—in full J cup glory.

"Oh…my…God," she says.

I've never been so comfortable with my body around another person. Especially not my husband. Maybe, it was the way I saw her face twinge with such a powerful desire to stare, not unlike what I've seen from men every so often for 20 years of carrying these bra breakers around. From the start, I was fascinated by the look; where I saw no jealously at all, but only the deepest amazement, which crushed her down to shyness and humility. Such a beautiful woman she is—golden light skin, jade green eyes and full, pink lips—one of the prettiest young women I've ever seen to tell the truth, with a tiny waist to accent hips so perfectly full and rounded as to create instant awe, with a set of breasts too firm and fair to be believed, considering their unusual heft, with all natural support, bound fully in the key of D Major, though still only a third as big as my own. I remember the feel of her firm nipple in my mouth in the kitchen, the feel of the soft, young breast over my tongue and against the roof of my mouth, which I sucked and moaned over like a starving child. So many times in our pre- ordination at the table, I let my dignity find its way out the door, with no worries as to when it would return—I had shook my head with her nipple in my mouth and bellowed like the sick, twisted cow that I am.

I stand at the mirror now fully exposed—topless and curved waisted, jeans *wet* in the front— hips tear-dropped to a smaller perfection than those on my new friend.

"You have a perfect body," she says. "Nova curved and everything."

"Nova… what?"

"There's a woman in the movie Planet of the Apes named Nova. She's a quiet, brunette beauty. Her waist has this deep, inward curve that I always remembered. You even have a great butt, too."

"You think so?"

"You're kidding, right?" She gets up from the comfortable chair, all tight t-shirt tits and tight jeans ass now, walking over to me. In the mirror, I see the reflection of a beautiful stranger stand behind me. The ghost in the mirror stiffens, enormous breasts hanging bulbous and low, shadowing the smooth hands sliding on the waist underneath them.

Somehow, from this plane of living, I hear the taller reflection in the mirror whisper to the shorter one, *Let's get you out of these wet pants*— the sound of which ignites the blue fire in my groin again—where the repression had broken and gushed from not too many minutes ago. The feel of this strange, smart, sexual woman nursing my breasts had sent a wave across the damned up river landscape and cracked it like the Grand Hoover at Armageddon, and what happened during my orgasm was enough to nearly make me pass out, sliding down through my groin like the rushing of a mighty stream—as so vulgar a spirit might whisper in regret: *"I came so hard I pissed myself,"* something I had never done before and truly, had never felt before. It was very nearly as it is written, 'an orgasm achieved with no apparent stimulus', though this Witch's Crown was certainly aided by her lips pulling at my nipples. I know that I have been touched by God himself, to have achieved a level of pleasure surely unknown to but few among us. But what calling is this? What reason for being is this unrighteous calling—to be destined to rest in the loving arms of a stranger?

She slides my pants completely off—the legs underneath, I see, are the same truth in advertising as what is in my blouse. My white legs are thick at the hips, especially at the sides, to complete the hourglass figure. Ignorance calls the fat on my thighs *saddlebags*, the dimpled skin *cellulite*—but those who know might see a shape aged to its perfect self by *hip pockets* and *jiggle* instead.

I watch and feel Austria Goldman slide my pants down and away. She stands up again slowly, her hands sliding up and over my hips more skillfully, with more desire than what my ridiculous husband ever had. She whispers directly in my year *"are you my Momma?"* I don't know what to say, but find myself nodding my head anyway. *"Are you my Momma now?"* I nod my head again. *"Let me hear you say it,"* she says. I mumble something or another—totally not to her satisfaction, I know. She takes both of my giant jugs in her hand and lifts them forcefully in one great and powerful squeeze—which pushes me further into my forbidden relaxation.

"Are you my daughter?" comes out of my spirit beneath consciousness, and I'm not sure if I heard it actually leave my mouth or not. *"Yes Momma,"* I hear her say, so I know I must have spoken the words—*"are you my daughter?"*

"Yes."

"Are you my Baby?"

"Yes, Momma."

The game relaxes me enough to lean my head further back with my face turned towards her, which she so skillfully meets with her warm lips and tongue on mine.

What private image are we! Two women bound to one another by Fate! One giant busted, topless in her underwear—the other still in her jeans standing behind—now pulling her white T shirt off above her head., then quickly removing her shoes and her jeans likewise.

She is closer behind me now—her arms wrapped tight around my waist. Then slowly, with inevitability, I feel her press her swollen groin against me—squeezing, releasing like a country mother in isolation about to paddle her daughter with a piece of wooden stick board. I can feel the bulge in her underwear—remarkable, where she is swollen to full blown womanhood. I sense the need—not so different from my own, and I push back against Lee Goldman at her groin.

She positions herself—with both hands grabbing my waist, and then she begins to pound my backside. Slowly at first, the authoress—taking her part of paradise offered. In the mirror I see an image of sinful beauty: the woman holding me bent over, my heavy breasts swinging down, her face now anguished over with the Dyke's Frustration, that she cannot grow herself to the fullness of a cock. This member she imagines—her own clitoris extended to a foot long inside me, to pound me into submission, and her into fervent domination. Her pounding becomes so forceful as to be masculine, unlike what I could have imagined from a woman—thrusting born from somewhere deep, energy charged from a lifetime of broken dreams.

Were this not a perverted part of herself, none of this would have happened, and I would be downstairs at the kitchen stove. But this fire burns a blue and black flame—it rises the heat of human wickedness, and whatever evils that must surely come.

She grunts deeply, that animal mating call so rare in women during carnality; where dignity is dismissed and abandon is welcomed in. This abandon I now feel in the both of us, as I am pushed back against her like a lioness in heat, to receive every inch of pounding and every pound of spirit force.

"Come for your Momma, Baby—come on that cock"—

This, with her panties rolled down below her buttocks—so she can feel them wiggle in the air. She is subject to the involuntary stroking of the brain—when the eyes roll back, and the voice does whatever it so desires, as I hear the grunting turn to a loud, hard shriek, causing me to look up in time to see her face twisted in agony—as she lowers her head in the aftermath of trauma.

$\mathcal{A}$utumn breezes flow the river of time. They rise and fall to encompass our fervent desire—to bring us hope for a new season—or to touch our souls in melancholy. These solemn days of Autumn have become part of who I am, more and more as a warning touch to my spirit, so that even in the spring or the summer, I often wonder what trials and tribulations, what troubles and tragedies lay ahead.

On the balcony of the upper room, I stand in my white robe of wealth and womanhood, overlooking the long path in front of the mansion home, and the row of cherry trees in the distance. I stand here, a woman unfulfilled—though having partook in the fulfillment of a lustful lifetime of dreaming. This fortnight of forbidden passion has seen me literally come and go with desire, and carnal attributes and abilities unknown.

My mind turns to the sleeping woman in my morning bed. Prompting a wondering in my unfrozen sensual mind; how many times in the two weeks since we've met have I stood at the edge of the big brown wood panel and post bed with my hands on my hips topless, or while she sat in chairs in a number of rooms including my daughter's room—how many times in two weeks have I stood with these nipples and mounds of flesh exposed, to be pinched, pulled and sucked to trembling?

The woman who holds this axe to grind—this angel of lascivious want and need—this minion of malevolent mischief lies asleep in the king sized bed and fine décor—every beautiful, bosomy inch of her lost in a far away dream. In something akin to disbelief, I turn away from the line of orchard trees, sure that I am awake and breathing, and gently open the door to peek inside from the Autumn cold. Almost to my surprise—there in reality is a woman I met two weeks ago lying asleep in my bed, eyebrows arched so incredibly over big, closed eyes and a perfect nose— big, pink lips relaxed in the Death Slumber. She lies on her side facing where I am, the sheets covering her up to her shoulders, in contrast to her lovely golden skin.

When she takes a deep breath of sleep and turns, I am twinged in my groin from the exotic nature of her look, and I am suddenly and strongly aware that she is not white, which overwhelms me with entitlement, and makes me want to possess her all the more. My groin suddenly aches with this revelation—this truth I have dared not dwell upon, because now I cannot help but feel slightly superior, and reaffirmed as the mistress of her life. I know that soon, I will be inside, underneath our sleeping shroud— laid on top of this woman as the female superior, her legs open underneath my hips, her tongue pulled deep in my mouth, while I hammer my message home to her groin. The Waltz of the Tribades will commence in the morn—on the Autumn breezes of this fervent September morn.

It rains on the just and the unjust—as Divinity is so inclined—that those who are wicked gather in the white rabbit field, to enjoy whatever merciful blessings that flow. And we count this privilege unto righteousness, believing that our blessings are the true favor of God. So many of us are in love with the Holy Scriptures, being able to quote this or that— from Genesis to Malachi, Matthew to Revelation, we love the Bible and profess to love the God of it, while we use the scriptures to justify our sin— believing that because we love the Bible, we love that selfsame God, believing it gives us the right to live any way we choose. *I'm a good person, I'm a good Christian,* we say, *God has blessed me because I live right*, we say. And we go on sinning without guilt, for how can we truly be guilty, when there is no Holy Spirit within, by which we might cause to grieve? And so, we go on about our white middle class and upper class way, loving the Bible and loving God, but loving him as a character in a story, and not as the Divine Creator, the one true and living God, who was once made flesh, and dwelt among us.

"Angels"
by Austria Goldman

"I remember my first whipping like it was yesterday. I can't recall if my father was dead or not. Mom said I was too young to remember when he died. But that whipping is as vivid as the blue sky on a cool summer's day, with a scattering of fluffy white clouds here and abouts. My mother was a Bible thumper even then. Even before we moved to the suburbs by way of white privilege, achieved easier perhaps, because my black father had died only a year before. But in the house on Bloomingdale Street, a little dead end nothing of a place in Williamston, NC, my earliest memory is of a belt whipping from my mother..."

And so pens my lover's confessional. A memoir of its author, so thinly disguised as fiction—of a single, suburban mother who abuses her daughter from childhood into her mid 30's, when the daughter finally snaps and stabs her mother to death on a cold, rainy Autumn night.

My mouth has hardly closed since I started reading—I don't know whether it is her smooth, easy prose style or the content of the prose itself, which makes no compromise as it chronicles the lengthy, nude belt whippings, both mother and daughter often unclothed, with the mother as remarkably voluptuous as I…

"… her big, long breasts swinging like bells back and forth with large, dark areolas on the white skin, above a small, fleshy waist pinched into a permanent and deep curve by the tight, high-waisted hose and underwear… every inch of her curvy body jiggles and wiggles in motion, which even through the blue and black flames I see, and I admire…"

Suddenly, I feel a lifting up, a new lightness come from nowhere, realizing it is Austria's hands sneaking up from behind over my robe—lifting up my bosom inside.

"Is it that bad?" she says.

"What?"

"Your eyes are misty. From the onions on that paper."

I only smile, and accept the over the robe chest massage, something I used to want to feel from my husband so many mornings but never did, going down the line in thought to the hands of our many friends so often. Soon, I feel her cold, smooth hand down the inside on my robe, as she works one of them slowly out. Leaning over my shoulder, she lifts my breast up and begins to nurse it hard and deep, pulling strongly enough to expect to taste morning milk down the back of her throat.

"The milk's in the kitchen," I say, which brings a full smile to her beautiful face, her teeth clamped on my nipple in the interim, which brings to mind a passage in her book I saw, where the daughter had…

"…imagined that there might be blood from [her] nipple this time…"

Unapologetically, still smiling a bit, Lee Goldman returns to the sucking. The deep nursing at my reading desk. My brain sends something good into my body.

"If you keep doing that, I'm going to cum again and I don't want to."

In only the kissing, pulling, smacking sounds that lead to the occasional slurping, she continues the fellatio of the nipple, which has a powerful affect on my body, which begins to chime inside when I remember the swinging of the angel mother's breasts in the book, while belt whipping her daughter's light skin to blood.

*L*ast night, I had a vision. A dream so vivid as to be photorealistic—indistinguishable from waking reality. There are no other details accept me on my knees on my bed, unclothed, Austria standing unclothed nearby. With her watching me, I notice that I have a *real penis* of equine stature between my legs, which is long enough for me to raise up between my own breasts, which I do—and I begin to stroke my own dick with my breasts, feeling the duality of pleasure, which is female perversion itself. I do this in smooth, bouncing rhythm while Austria looks on in something like anguished amazement, watching me on my knees stroke myself with my own gigantic bosoms. I open my eyes, just long enough to see the woman in the mirror shoot the thickness from her own cock onto her breasts in travail and trembling, which as I begin to cry out from the unbearable pleasure—I realize that the woman is *me*.

As I escort the lovely blonde Susan Marshall from the front door to the kitchen table, the vision of my dream self plagues the theater of my mind.

Susan Olivia Marshall. Forty eight years of repressed curves—all packed into a pair of Spanx underneath her gray business suit. Piercing, pretty blue eyes underneath the blonde, corporate haircut. Eyes careworn with knowledge of good and evil. Hips full with the pride of this life— strong, shapely white legs under the skirt veil—stepped smartly onto heels of judgment and hypocrisy.

She steps lively through her own *fungalooga* smile, that grin of practiced phoniness and chatter—barely a millionaire herself, but enough so as to walk in the presence of designated dealings of destined decadence and depravity. An inner soul of corruption. Masked by courteous and cultured civility.

She walks beside me in smiles and chatter, as if she belongs. As if she were the best friend I've ever had, as if at will, she could rise to another station of prominence and being.

"It's the *only* way books get published Honey... I told you that before. The book industry has tried to undergo some silly metamorphosis to box office style product, with sales and money as the only real object," she says. "But the truth is that in the age of TV and internet, people just aren't buying books like they used to. And it still comes down to who likes what and why. And if the truth be told, it's even worse with literary agents, the very ones who were supposed to have changed the industry for the better, have nepotised and self-served the novel industry nearly to death. Its why I'm not an agent anymore. I don't know how many brilliant novels I rejected because I wasn't sure if they'd sell. It was our job to find an author we could market whether or not the book was worth a damn; unless somebody in the agency really liked it then it didn't matter, which turned out to be the case most of the time anyway. Sometimes I think we'd have done better if we had just closed our eyes and shot paint balls at the slush pile. We were always looking for the next Terry Goodkind or J.K. Rowling—somebody with a catchy name and a stack of hot books to sell. It was our job to spot so called literary books—good books with deep, and in some cases inspired, soulful writing. It was our job to catch these books like a jungle anaconda and chop it up into a million pieces."

"Susan, you're not serious."

"As a heart attack, Baby. *Chop that elephant up*, we used to say. The age of the literary artist is dead. Writers with a calling to one dead book, obviously inspired, some even outstanding with flashes of brilliance, but with no hope of earning anybody enough money for it to matter. I've had to kill some the most beautiful little books. We called 'em literary bombs. A literary artist is as easy to spot as a giraffe in a wheat field. And just as easy to kill. When I was an agent, whatever junk we could sell is what we represented. And literary novels aren't selling. You wouldn't believe the amount of novels we reject from literary agents nowadays. In all honesty, one of the reasons I became an editor is so I can help some of these brilliant books find a home. I believe there's still a place for art in the literary world. Money isn't everything."

"I'm so glad to hear you say that. I believe this girl's book *is* art, Sue. It moved me like nothing I've ever read. Of course, I'm not an expert… I've only read a few novels in my whole life. But this…it … *feel*s like a work of art to me. But if the industry really is changing… I mean, she found it impossible to get an agent, I'll let her tell you what she went through with those literary agents. It's heartbreaking."

Susan glances into her memory. A quick, plaintive stare, head shaking, eyes burdened by pity—be it real or manufactured, I do not know.

"Evil and complacent."

"What?"

"It's what an author accused me of being, right before I sold the agency and became an editor. The book industry is changing alright… for the *worse*. And literary agents are the biggest reason why. And greedy, jaded, shortsighted book editors, too… I've seen it. So, I guess we're all to blame. Where's your author?"

"She couldn't… Sue, the truth is she didn't want to blow it. She said she wanted you to judge the book on its own merits. She said writers should be read and not seen—whatever that means."

"*Angels* by Austria Goldman. Austria Goldman. Little bit of a ring there, isn't it?"

"I keep trying to tell her that. She's one of those rare cases… somebody really pretty and really nice who's… really shy."

"Really?"

We share a brief, un-awkward smile. Politeness—practiced to perfection.

"Have you actually read the whole book?" she asks.

"When you read it, you'll know why it's so important to her."

"What did you think of it? Really?"

I take the deepest breath possible—unashamed of my bosom's epic rise and fall.

"Must be pretty hot," she says. "I'll just… read it myself."

"So, this is the real thing, right Sue? You'll publish it?"

"Don't you worry," she says, rising to her feet. "It's in the right hands."

I ignore the pressure inside. That drive to push for another question. In keeping with those who have risen to her level in the business world—a straight answer to a question about her own commitment to a project is impossible. In the same fungalooga happiness as before—this time from me—we walk back through the living room to the front door—her with the controversy in her leather bag, me with the awkward anticipation in my heart.

"Sue… I really appreciate this favor… and I intend to make it worth your while. I just want to make sure I'm not giving Austria false hope, you know. I want to be able to guarantee her that this is it."

"Well…the truth is, Sarah, nothing is certain in the book business, but tell your friend not to worry, okay? I'll come back by tomorrow morning, say around this same time."

"We'll be here."

Bells of intuition chime the morning hour, those of instinct and premonition. Even though I am deeply acquainted with the so-called rightest of right people to get my job done, I feel as lost as a traveler stranded in the middle of a desert after dark, with only the stars and a cold night wind for comfort. There was no commitment whatsoever forthcoming, and I know now that Fate decides over reason, and Destiny overrides indecision. The feelings that the book gave me are paramount, but might go unfiltered through another, uncushioned by affection and compassion for the author, for the two weeks that I have known her. Is it possible for me to have had an unbiased reading of every atrocity and abomination inside? It never occurred to me, through the one day it took for me to read the mother–daughter story, that if I had come across this in a bookstore, I would probably have dismissed the book as trash.

At the top of the stairs, Lee stands quietly. Looking down at me.

How can we reconcile ourselves to the Lord, for all the things we are, and wherewithal for such things as we have done! I vow—as I think after the woman who has come and gone, and upon the beautiful woman above me, I know that there are curses made that encompass the generations—from the seed and sapling root, to the top branches of our most fervent family tree. I gaze the loveliness of this hopeful anticipation, standing against the banister high above me as the lustful fruit of this generation, wondering in full by which it cometh; of what manner of fruit this tree hath blossomed over time—whether it be good, or whether it be evil.

"I assume you heard everything."

"Actually, no. I was too afraid to listen. I came out when I heard you at the door."

I continue to be drawn upward, as though by a force emanating. I take the stairs gladly up towards her, like a wayward flying swan to a jet engine fan.

"My bruises never really bother me when I go to school—I'm never really shy about them. Socially, I'm well adjusted enough; what I see in the mirror is sexy and pretty enough to keep Eva Watson from deluding me too much about it. I'm as pretty as every cheerleader. But the one thing I don't have in common with them concerns the happiness allele, which they have in great abundance. They don't bother me too much, because I'm not antisocial—but I'm tall enough and busty enough to cause a little trepidation among my peers, especially since I'm not involved in a single club or activity. My refuge is my grades—my studies—which I think has saved me from ostracization, being that not since I was in the sixth grade has my report card seen anything less than an A minus.

I guess I learned early to try as hard as I could not to give her a reason to be angry, starting with my grades at school, because for so many years they were a focal point of contention—being locked in my room without supper and forced to study instead of eat—where crying and defiance were sent so many times to die—for if I were to huff and holler she would burst into the room and put me over her knee and spank bruises onto my naked bottom until her bare hands were so ~~sore~~ raw she couldn't do it anymore.

I think this is the memory that burns me up now between classes, in the burning of my skin from this morning's violence, having been graduated to the wood of a hairbrush. I was beaten this morning because I was accused of being 'sassy' with her. She had rushed into the bathroom and pulled my hair hard enough to make me hear violin music. Then she had let me go and told me to come to her bedroom—which I did so un-gradually this morning, so un-casually I walked behind her, the same way I walk behind this teacher who won't get out of my way. I can remember the feel of my jeans coming off in my mother's bedroom, which irritated me something fierce because the fit was so perfect. My mother too—in a fog of quiet, unreasoning rage, *too,* her own clothes off down to her bra and panties— her bra being so ridiculously large to have to hold those big, swinging bells in place. This morning, this first day of my 9th grade year—is it a benchmark in my psychological development   (arrest), I wonder with each step toward the strange and new classroom, in easy command already because of my face and body and big smile and skin the color of Jordin Sparks—yes, I am one of the elite in this school, in that I have a secret that can never be told, that this morning I graduated from a hard spanking to a hairbrush, which took place standing up in front of the mirror, where I was able to see my mother's face twisted in a somber anguish and frown, while her arm worked as tirelessly as the giant pistons in the Titanic, with her other hand clumsily across my mouth to contain my screaming.

This morning, yes, I became a member of the elite—those who have seen their mother's naked breasts exposed in anger—when I watched her undress down to her underwear, then take off her big bra un-ashamedly, then tell me to stand still at the mirror and to hold on to the dresser. My screaming had been so loud as to make her furious, until she mashed her snow white hand to my lips and beat bruises from my ass down to the back of my knees.

As I sit down, yes, my *ass* (rather than my bottom) is sore because I am angry, and I wonder if any one of these girls have ever even been whipped a day in their lives…"

Susan Marshall burns with desire. Susan Marshall. Typically repressed. Bound by hypocrisy. Feelings buried deep in the puritanical mind. The bureaucratic heart. Feeling awakened by the words she cannot stop reading under cloak of night. In the wealthy suburbs somewhere in Connecticut, safe in Brick Mansion luxury. One year of her lawyer husband's $700,000 dollar salary—bought and paid for by privilege. Years of struggle—the hardness of heart. The emotions of the high upper middle class buried deep. A stone monument of Death—sensibilities so fragile—sworn to kill all threats to the mentality. To the way of life.

Locked in her study—kids and husband playing somewhere in time—in the vicinity of she. Locked in her study—comfortably unclothed. Unbroken. Unmoved. Unbelieving. Unmerciful. Unwilling. Uncompromising. Unashamed.

Susan Olivia Marshall. Keeper of the Gates of Reason. Waiting over the Barrier of Time. The *nude* warrior in her study. Unafraid. Untouched. Unkind to the slithering serpent of truth in the Goldman pages. Unaffected. Unresisting. Held captive by the bureaucratic mentality. Unaware. Allowing herself to be burned by what she reads. By the blue and black fire within. Flames she is charged by Fate to extinguish. Truths too dark to release. Too volatile to unleash. Too menacing to oblige. Susan Marshall. Ablaze. On fire from the mother and the daughter. Unrepentant.

Unholy.

It is a sea of lily white, with the occasional tulip and yellow rose in bloom. This Sunday afternoon of wealthy and privileged shoppers mill around us in the mall; the sights, sounds and smells of luck and money. Young faces, middle aged faces of coin and culture—happy teenagers un-introduced to poverty, want and need—girls and boys bored with life even before graduating from high school, their mothers jaded to the beeping sound of swiped credit cards, the smell of new clothes and cars, the hustle and feel of plastic bags bustled about, heavy with the lust of the eyes—filled with the pride of life. All of them bound by consumerism, the need to be enticed to spend exorbitant sums of money, while begrudging the trumpet sounds of charity.

Today, Austria Goldman is one of them. With me comfortably, richly by her side—as abundant a source for her to drink from as that for a deer at a clear and trickling stream. All day, back to yesterday evening, from when Susan Marshall took the manuscript from my hands—I have resisted and pushed and fought against the question that flashes the theatre of my mind.

"She's you, isn't she?"

Her look is a masterpiece of false bewilderment. "Who's me?"

"Emily. The girl in your novel."

Her big lips are suddenly tucked in, pressed to hide the embarrassment, the humiliation of discovery. Which is a bit of a surprise to me really, because I would think she would know how thinly veiled her story and characters really are.

"She's not really me," she says, putting the folded jeans back in their gap against the wall. "She's how I felt growing up. She punished me a few times, but it…"

When our eyes, meet, there is the sudden realization that there need be no secrets between us. No places where we have gone that need hiding from the other, nowhere in the abiding desert dark our lives have been.

Sometimes, in the single breath of a phrase—*"Let's go home"*—there is the impending answer to so many questions, like the dawn before a rising sun. We hardly say a word on our little trek through the busy mall—though what a pair we must surely be! A middle aged white woman of 45, heavy-chested as the most deviant Dolly Parton dream, though nearly hidden under the black cable knit sweater and white t shirt, to give motherly contrast to my 32 year old companion—who does not hide her figure in the long sleeve turtleneck shirt and jeans. How far away from their mind's idea we must be—an older business woman I am to them, with my lowly assistant rolling beside me. A professor I must be, my bust making me appear top heavy and misshapen in the black cable knit, white t shirt and gray pants. Who is the puff breasted store manager walking fast through the mall, with her pathetic underemployed assistant manager in tow! What animosities lie between them! What career destruction lies beneath a frown! Who is the granny breasted CEO, called down from her office in the clouds, dragging her corporate assistant around in servitude! What school does the Parton-breasted one principal, what unlucky children are they!

"My earliest memory is of a whipping," she says. In the autumn gray and cold, the car is truly a refuge as I drive. It wasn't until I left the big parking lot behind was this epic silence broken. The relief floods my body like warm water.

"I don't remember my father," she says. "I just remember... I remember a man in my mother's bed one night when I was little. I must have been really young because I could see them through the white bars in my crib. I don't remember the man at all except that he was there. But my mother was naked—I can see it plain as day. She was laid on her side towards the man. Then she turned over—and her breasts flopped and wobbled the whole time. And then I remembered I swallowed a nickel—and I almost choked on it, but I swallowed it. It hurt my throat. Then I felt it slide all the way down into my stomach. Maybe that's my earliest memory. My Momma's tits while I swallowed a nickel in my crib."

The sound of her voice lights the Theatre of My Mind. Where memories and suppositions are brought to life. From the sound of my lover's voice—energy flows to where it may form an image for me to see. In the drone of my lover's voice, there is the power of a beautiful woman she once knew—a white woman of beauty and blonde hair, with large dark eyes, perfect nose and lips, with a sultry voice capable of a man's bass—stature every bit of five feet ten, her golden hair slicked back into a French braid, bun, ponytail or Indian braid—but always pulled back away from a face of extraordinary perfection and sensuality. A woman named Laura Ingrid Stone—Goldman by a forbidden marriage to a man named Mark, phenotyped as non-white, whose skin bore the African night. Her loving black husband, who she mourned and grieved with every turning of the day, the passing of every season, upon every revolution of the heavenly sphere—she grieved Mark Goldman's passing. And buried so deep inside that grief was the seed of anger, compounded by the infidelities he committed, magnified by the Death he wrought, done by the hands of one of his mistresses—shot in the head while he slept fully clothed on the young mistress' bed, as he had endeavored to break his adulterous pattern.

Mark, Marcus Goldman rests in peace. In uneasy peace, having left a white widow behind, and a four year old daughter cursed by the hopeless name Austria Lee. Laura and Lee Goldman. Daughter, granddaughter of a North Carolina state appellate court Judge (Wallace Stone, we'll call him), who had forbade his nineteen year old daughter to marry that "black son of a bitch." Who was so incensed by his daughter's marriage to him while she was in college that he cut her off like a Doberman's tail, and refused to let her in the door of his home, let alone her voice through the speaker of his phone. Add to all of this, a four year old mix breed, hi-yellow and half white bitch she didn't know whether to call 'Austria' or 'Lee'. Had she not loved Mark, it would have made no difference that he was gone. But between his adulteries, his death, and her own father's denial of her, inside were the beginnings of a rumbling spirit quake—that threatened to rain debris down and around the daughter she despised.

I see Laura Goldman upon the Theatre of My Mind. Beautiful, lost in a post apocalypse, tears on her beautiful face, holding a little gray child by the hand. And though Laura has given her heart and mind to the Baptist Church, the seed of hatred still burns for the happiness she was denied, and the fire often burns every inch of her daughter's skin. And none of these arrows that breach her sanity have made her aware of it—even while behind the southern Christian façade, as she takes a pound of retribution from her daughter's mind and body. Yes—I see the legendary *Mord Sith* drag the little girl by the hair, as efficiently as a hawk holds a condemned rabbit in her claw—dragging her down the hall to one of her earliest belt whippings—and the first one that she will remember.

The Baptist beauty closes the bedroom door and removes every stitch of the little girl's clothing in conjunction with her own—and proceeds to belt whip the little girl to hoarse and heavy screams, while she herself begins to pray to God for the strength to carry out this little girl's training—this rambunctious and mischievous little devil, who deserves to be chastised to within an inch of her little life, for talking back will never be discussed or tolerated, only dealt with in the swiftest and most brutal fashion. And the feeling in Laura's body—the deep and abiding heat waves that course through, which began when she began to disrobe as though inspired—these waves are called upon, to course through her body as a sign to her, that if she beats her child with the rod of discipline—she shall not die, but shall instead be rescued from the fiery pits of Hell. And in private, behind the closed doors of working class suburbia—the child's screams ignite sensations in her body that are fed by the *whap, whap, whapping* of the strapping on her skin, and even the feel of her own breasts swinging and wiggling free before the Lord. For this, Laura Stone counts as righteousness, as her mother before her, ad nauseam up the family tree back to Mother Russia and the origins of the Ingrid byname. Laura Ingrid Stone—a.k.a. Laura Goldman, discovers the Marquis gene in her own body, coursing through her blood, activated by the screams and every lash, until the rhythm of the whipping sends mercy packing for hills, and every stroke of the belt massages her flesh to moisture and tingling. *"Stupid, hardheaded, little nigger bitch* is the coda of this grand overture which hath washed through her body to completion, swelling an unknown energy from her groin outward, which makes her pick the little girl up and slam her on the bed face down, then sit astraddle her little buttocks and listen to the crying die down to sobbing. Then, the energy in her body flares up to push pretense beyond the walls of secret, and Laura Stone lies down on top of the little girl—draped over her, pushed down heavy on top of her—to where her groin begins the involuntary slamming up and down, until the girl's quiet sobbing voice is soon joined by her own.

In my ears, from the reality of time and memoriam, I hear a woman cry out in physical and spiritual pain—that caused by a pleasure far too intense and fearful to bear.

$\mathcal{T}$he cold of this early autumn has crept inside—to put me in mind of winter days ahead. The days of Austria begin to fade into the weeks of her, until early autumn lapses into Indian summer, and the colorful death of every deciduous leaf in Creation. Long past these empty promises, these hours of false hope in lying warmth and false light—long past these lying summer days we roll on by, to the rolling highways of November's impassioned arrival. My husband has come and gone again—a million blessed miles away in his billion dollar life and mistress wife, living with another woman somewhere outside of my line of sight as if she were his own. Of this, I choose not to know, nor do I choose to care. I suppose he has grown tired of my gargantuan breasts, and the pressure to perform they provide. His newfound absenteeism could not have come at a better time in my life—giving me more than a little satisfaction that now, I just don't need him anymore, except to keep funneling financial fuel into this lonely lifestyle I'm in.

On my bedroom balcony, overlooking the row of cherry trees, this pre-winter cold shows me the tip of an iceberg in my memory. I first saw it way back in September, adrift on the icy waters of Austria's recall. She told me that her mother had stripped her naked when she was four, threw her on the bed like a wrinkled sheet and then laid her own naked body on top of her little daughter and humped herself into a voice like a siren. Like an ice mountain, this Truth of Cataclysm rose high into the gray sky, adrift along the icy current in frozen grandeur. But as big and as spectacular as this revelation may have been, it truly is only the tip of the iceberg, with the unseen spreading out as big as a mountain underneath.

"She said she was coming over this afternoon," Lee says, closing the balcony door behind her. "I think this is it. I can feel it. I could feel it all day—something really big is about to happen. I can't believe it—I'm really going to be a published writer. I owe it all to you, Sarah."

Lee steps up behind me, squeezing me around the waist, looking off into the distance with me. In my heart, I can feel the flow of time and history, that moved this woman past the gate of my lawn almost two months ago. I can only wonder if these feelings will pass, the stir of tranquility she brings to my spirit. Oh, but who do I think I am, Oh Lord, to exploit the abomination inside her! To draw her into my own desire for female perversion! Am I as guilty as her mother had been? How am I not guilty of abusing her naiveté, her need to have me in her life? What would she do if I were to pull the brakes on this train, to where the wheels go screaming, as I throw her overboard into a rolling heap of nothing?

"I think you must really be meant to be a writer. You've been here for two months and you haven't asked me for anything."

"I haven't written anything either. I tried the other day, but I can't. It's bigger than writer's block, which never really happens to me."

"It's my fault, isn't it? I'm a hindrance. And a distraction."

She turns me around to face her. Pressing my backside hard against the railing.

"Oh, but what a distraction indeed."

She moves such a beautiful face to mine until my eyes are closed—and I feel a tingle in the body electric, and the softness of her lips pressed to mine. I am a woman, yes, but so too is Lee Goldman, a woman named Austria, who lights me up like gray clouds in a winter lightning storm. Yes, as rare and special as that, because such a thing is possible under the sun.

"I need to ask you something." My voice is quiet. Almost whispery. "Did you ever kiss your mother like that?"

"All the time."

The words slide into my body and down my spine—where I feel them spread energy to my buttocks and groin. "I'm sorry."

"Does it turn you on to hear that?" she says.

"Yes. I swear to God, I tried as hard as I could not to let it get to me. But it does. I've been wanting to ask you about it for weeks."

"Mother-daughter incest?"

"Yes."

"You want to know did I fuck my mother."

"Yes."

She reaches down deep in the dyke soul, and plants a man sized kiss on my lips hot enough to melt the snows of this coming winter. Taking one last drink of her tongue in my mouth, I imagine that I am Laura Stone, taking my part of my daughter's hope and chastity.

I finally suck away from the kiss, and take deep and shameful breath.

"I'm sorry, Austria. Please forgive me."

"For what?"

"I feel like I'm using you."

"Using me?" she says.

I push her away gently, strolling to the other side of the balcony. "What are we doing?"

"Living, Honey."

"But how are we living?" I say. "Is any of this real? We'd hardly known each other for an hour and we were—" I see the delight in her eyes. Waiting for me to speak of what is done in secret. "I can't even say it."

"Are you done with me already?"

"What?"

"I knew it was too good to be true," she says. "Beautiful, rich woman like you. What would you want with a piece of trash like me?"

She tries to be light, as though she wants me to feel manipulated and to *not* take her seriously. But beneath the smirk and relaxed posture, her arms folded, I can see that her toughness is as fragile as a crystal rose figurine.

"I just don't want to be responsible for hurting you, Lee. This ridiculous life of mine—"

"You called me Lee."

"I did?"

"Yeah," she says, slightly amazed.

"This is Paradise, Lee. It's a touch of Heaven on Earth. It's got me set up so I can go anywhere in the world—buy anything in the world, and *that* gives me security. If you were to spit in my face and run off and never come back, I'd get over it because of all this money. Success is the greatest anti-depressant in the world. I don't need pills and a glass of wine because when I start fantasizing about the grave, I just go online and click, click, credit card *click,* and I can survive another day. And if push *does* come to shove, I do have my stupid husband and his damned children to see to. Playing billionaire wife and mother does give me something to do. But what about you, Baby? What if your book doesn't sell? What would you do if the world rejects you as a writer? What if I throw you out on your ass right now, what would you do? Where would you go? Do you know you haven't been home once in the two months since you've been here? If what we have is just a fling, Honey, I don't want to see you get hurt. And if you are manipulating me with a bunch of lies—if you are just using me as a place to crash until you get your book published, I want you to respect me enough to tell me now before we go any further."

"I want you to be honest, Sarah. Are you asking me to leave?"

I let the bewilderment in my eyes do the talking.

"I mean… you've been different since your husband came back."

"Have I?"

"I didn't want to say anything, but you have. Is it because he was weird about me staying here?"

"Trust me, he could care less about that. With your looks, Honey, he would've tried to bang you himself if he was here long enough."

"What is it, then?"

"I just feel like I'm taking over your life, Lee."

"And why is that such a bad thing?"

"Because you don't need anybody holding you down ever again—keeping you from living the life you want to live. I don't want you to feel obligated to me because of this book thing."

"Is that what you think?" she asks. "I'm using you, or that you're obliging me?"

"What else can it be, Austria? You're not going to tell me that you love me, are you?"

"Austria," she says. "I… I feel like… like I don't need anything when I'm here with you. Like I've already been given my heart's desire. So what if you're a busty brunette beauty, with tits enough to satisfy a lifetime of mother-daughter issues in me. Even if she hadn't done those thing to me, I'd still be banging you, sweetie. Hell, you turn me on so much, Sarah, you make me want to grow a cock sometimes."

"Like you felt when your mother took her clothes off in front of you, right?"

"What?"

"You heard me. Just tell the truth about it. I remind you of your mother."

"My mother did *not* have tits like that."

"It's not about my tits, Austria. It's about real security and comfort. I meet your emotional needs for the moment, and that's why you're doing this, I know it. I have no right to take advantage of that."

In her expression, I see the depressive spirit rise and fall, to betray profound disappointment, the echo of pain—and the despair she has always known. How lost, how devastated must she feel, to have been told by me in so many words—*hey bitch, you fucked your mother! get lost!* I know that somehow, I have done the very thing to her I swore to God and Jesus I would never do.

"Please forgive me," I say, hugging her tight to my bosom. The powerful hurt in her spirit, the devastation on her face... I know I caused it. And her pain is now mine.

"Are you gonna leave now?"

"I can't," she says. "I love you."

Susan Marshall rides the wind. The winds of earthly progression. In Lexus luxury, she cruises the Wealthen Stream. Grieving for the Land of Plenty. From six weeks ago, and the nude reading of the Goldman papers. Her introduction to the truth. From six weeks ago, when sensibilities were awakened—those she had not seen before. When possibilities rise and fall before her very eyes, amidst the Dreams of Avarice—literary prestige, fame and fortune for a young author. Susan Marshall moves along the timeline—on the energy of what she believes. In the power of what she knows. Thereby flows the Will of God and Man, and the inevitable course of events. The Chaos of Living. The tranquility of dying. The brutality of Consequences, and the outcome of choices made.

Inevitability rides in luxury.

Unguilty.

"Here. Take a look at this."

In our grand living room, waiting for Fate to come knocking, she hands me a faded color photo of a woman on the beach, lost somewhere in time and history. Fully noticeable in the inexplicably avocado two piece are hips of extraordinary curve from the tiniest waist, with a pair of cantaloupe sized low riders hanging bulbous in the loose string bikini top.

"Is this your mother?"

"No. It's my grandmother. My Mom's mother."

Marveling how it is that the 70's seem to photograph differently from every other decade, I stare deep into an Ashley Judd faced woman of substance and sensuality, with a smile as rich and full as her hourglass figure. I see nothing of what was passed down in her expression—not a hint of the depressive spirit, nor echo of the divine negativity within.

"That's your body alright. I think I can even see her in your face. You're like an exotic version of her."

"Mom said she was a manic depressive bitch, who swung back and forth like a clock pendulum."

"She looks so happy."

"This, I'm sure was one of her good swings."

"Do you think she abused your mother?"

"I don't think she did, I know she did. But it was so secret, my grandfather didn't even know it. All he knew about was the occasional belt whipping and hard paddling. She was a housewife and church lady. While my grandfather was out chasing judge's robes and rainbows, my grandmother was home locked in a bedroom with her oldest daughter. Mom once told me that when she was 11 years old, she remembers spanking her mother's naked ass in the bedroom—"

"Oh, my *God*." For some reason, my hand is over my mouth.

Why?

"Right. Imagine hearing something like that when you're in the 5th grade."

"Austria, you're not serious."

"I was in the fifth grade, when Mom told me her mother would stand still with her eyes closed and her wrists tied in front, with her hands pressed still against her stomach, you know, kinda low just above her yoo-ha. And she would make Mom spank her until her little hands hurt. Mom's mother, this woman here, would just stand there with her legs together, eyes closed. Concentrating. They did this more than once when my Mom was eleven. She told me that one Sunday morning when her father was out of town, they were getting ready to go to church when she called Mom to her room. And she took Mom's clothes off."

"The woman in the picture," I say. "She made your mother do this when she was eleven."

"Yep. I know you don't believe me but that's okay, I wouldn't expect you to. Naked eleven year old Mom then took all of her mother's clothes off, tied her mother's wrists with her *bra*. *"Hit me as hard as you can,"* she said. Mom said that when she hit her, her mother told her to stop. But then her ass shook and squeezed, then her whole body shook. She said her mother made a sound like a cow being branded."

"Oh, Jesus," I say. "Oh, Lord. What does that do to a child? And this happened to your mother Laura when she was a little girl?"

"Unless Laura was lying to me for ten years. "

"What's your grandmother's name?"

"Helen. Helen Ingrid Stone. Helen Ingrid Komar. Helen Ingrid Komarovski."

"Komarovski?"

"Her parents were Russian. God only knows what her mother did to her. To them."

"Who's them?"

"She was the youngest of four girls—Helen was the only one born here. Grew up and married old Judge Wallace Stone, my grandfather. Passed the middle name Ingrid down to her daughter Laura, the little girl with the magic spank. My mother."

"God forgive me for asking this, but did it ever happen again? Did Helen ever... well..."

"Cum again?"

Suddenly, I'm unable to speak.

"I don't know."

"Your mother didn't pass *that* down, did she?"

"She was busy passing down something else," Austria says.

"So… if I'm clear… this beautiful, normal looking, Chapel Hill suburbs living housewife, married to a judge, had her own 11 year old daughter *spank her to orgasm* in private."

By now, I suppose my anguished bewilderment is epic.

"That's why things like that will never go away. Because it's just too unbelievable. And too much a part of humanity. And it gets people where they live—it touches them too deep. I think it's one of the biggest signs of the times. The revelation of private sin. It's a sign that the end of the world is coming. The things we do to our children behind closed doors."

I am transfixed by the Ingrid Doll in the picture. Refusing to accept that this woman ever even had such *thoughts*.

"What does it do to a child? What affect does something like that have on a little girl. I mean… I *never* saw my mother naked, and there wasn't even the suggestion of anything close to that in my house. My tits were twice as big as my mommas when I was eleven, and she showed no interest in them whatsoever. In my house it was like they were just a normal part of my life. It was *outside* the house where I found out my breasts weren't normal. I got picked at so badly in school I wanted a breast reduction. But as I got older I started to understand how special they were."

"Because of men?"

"I hate to admit it, but mostly, yeah. I couldn't go anywhere, or do anything without getting stared at. Even the prettiest women acted really jealous when I came around. By the time I graduated from college I had just accepted it. Truth is they made me more confident. And I stopped hiding them. Funny thing is, as soon as I started to own my body for what it was, people started treating me a little differently. I kind of felt sorry for 'em because sometimes they acted just plain scared of me. But behind my back and when I wasn't looking they snickered and laughed at me like I was a naked circus clown. Let me ask you something Austria… What was your honest, first reaction when you first saw me?"

"I got thirsty for a glass of milk."

"Really?"

"No… no, I'm just kidding."

"What did you really think?"

"I was so scared, I didn't really notice until we started walking towards the house. And when I realized how big you were up top—it was like… like seeing a Bengal tiger in person, and then being denied a second look. My entire body was in agony to stare."

"I understand. The tiger analogy is interesting. I guess I do belong in a circus."

"In our bedroom circus, Baby. My naked clown."

In my smile, there is still the flash of realization of who she is, and what life it is she led.

"So what we have here is a genuine, real life survivor. A survivor of mother-daughte —I can't even say it."

"See? Even after the things we've done together. Even after our own deep perversion—you still can't face the truth. You still can't accept it. In your mind, I'm just some crazy, dyke con artist with no talent and no future, who has duped you with the sickest, most unbelievable story you've ever heard. You can't accept it, even though you've told me that your daughters have hardly ever been paddled by you when you weren't topless. Even though the perversion is a part of you, you still can't accept the fullness of it. The third part of the truth. Which is cataclysm."

She takes the picture from me, then straddles me on the couch—pushing full against me. Her eyes are azure in green.

"Who do you belong to?" she says. I honestly don't know what to say. Have I ever truly been spoken to in this manner? Truly? She takes a clump of my hair into her hand. And she pulls. Painfully. "I asked you a *question,*" she says, loudly enough to scare me, so that her voice carries through the house. "Who do you belong to?"

"I belong… I belong to you."

"That's right," she says. "You do. And you're my new *Mom,* aren't you?"

"Yes."

"Say it."

"I'm your new Momma."

"That's not what I said. I said *Mom.*"

"I'm your new… Mom."

"Say it like you *mean* it!"

"I'm your new *mother!*"

"I said *MOM!*"

"I'm your new *MOM!*"

The sound of fear flows around us, delivered so clearly from my voice into the world. Deep inside her stare, is the razor's edge. The sharp and clearly defined edges of a repressed and deeply controlled rage. The burning of blue and black fire.

"And tonight, you know what's gonna happen to you? Tonight, I'm gonna make my new mother cum. My new mother's gonna cum on her daughter's cock."

Her new authority plays deeply in her voice, to where I am amazed at how fearful I have become. Listening to the deep, masculine power coming through a woman's voice.

"What's going to happen to you?"

"I'm going to cum."

"On what"

"On my daughter's cock."

"Say the whole thing."

She suddenly pulls my hair hard enough that I see a lavender haze. "Oww… I'll come on my daughter's cock!"

I hear the pitiful, defeated tone of my loud voice—my head pain suddenly relieved, my vision a watery haze now, her lips pressed to mine in mercy. When I close my eyes, the watery haze coalesces, and runs down my face in a single tear.

"You alright?"

"Yeah," I say, sniffing, wiping my eyes.

"I thought you were into it, Babe."

"I was, I am, believe me. It's just that… you kinda scared me there for a second."

"Really?"

"Yeah."

"I scared you, huh?"

I nod my head pathetically, tucking my lips. Staring at her jade ocean eyes.

"I'll make it up to you later," she says.

"Okay. But like you said… I'm your Mom, right?"

"Yes."

"Then as your Momma, I think that your behavior towards me was... inappropriate. And before I ... *'cum on your cock,'* as you say... I think you need to be reminded that you are the daughter. I am the mother. Is that right?"

"Yes, Maam."

"I'm going to treat you like I would any daughter of mine who oversteps their bounds. I'm going to punish you."

I see the humility, the meekness—the echo of distant longing in her eyes again.

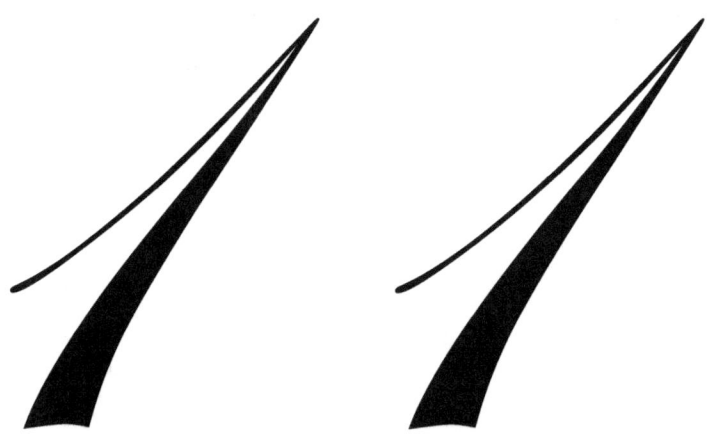

*I*t is written, that people never punish righteously. They do it out of sinful, sadistic urges. An inherent need to make other people suffer. Discipline, thy name is pain.

What we do, we must do it quickly. Even as the hour approaches—as Susan Marshall cruises the miles toward where we wait—the black fire of violence has ignited in my body—and I walk my charge quietly up the long staircase, then with purpose down the upstairs hall to our refuge, inside the upper room. The air inside is still, where grows the same tension I have felt many times over the years. From a special place inside my closet, I remove the large, Brownwood paddle, stained by invisible sweat, blood, and years of pain and suffering.

"Now… I want you to take off your clothes. Every stitch, and place them neatly on the bed. I want you to know that I love you, and I'm glad for your impending success… but none of it matters unless you learn respect for your mother. Not the woman who brought you screaming into this world, but your new mother. Me."

I watch her take her jeans off, ashamedly, to reveal the remarkable hips underneath, which I must concede as what only the inevitable must declare: as the gloriously full and rounded *ass* underneath, which is soon exposed fully to me. At long last, she takes off her bra that remains, and though she tries to hide it, I see the abject humiliation on her face, and the hint of genuine sorrow and defeat in her eyes.

"I want you to understand," I say, lifting my already cleavage-showing blouse up and over my head, "that punishment is an act of love. You think I'm going to say that I don't want to do this. But on the contrary, I *do* want to do this. I *have* to do this."

I reach around to the back of my boulder holding bra, unlatching it and letting it slip away from what lies beneath, feeling gravity take a large and heavy hold. In my jeans, topless—I pick up the paddle and walk towards the now frightened young woman, whose eyes betray the deep apprehension in her spirit. The black fire in my body is suddenly tinted blue, from my bowels upward, until with one hand I pull both my nipples one quick time in full view, to establish my comfort level, and absolute authority over her.

"I want you to prepare yourself, because this is not for pleasure. This is for correction, and I promise you it's going to hurt. Your job is to stand here and take it until I'm done. Now, turn around, put your hands on top of your head, feet together. Stand up straight—do not squeeze your buttocks together. I am your new mother, Austria. And you will respect me."

Without further warning, I wallop the fat of her backside hard enough to make her strain to repress a loud yell. With only one swat of the wooden board, I am delighted to see the shape of it marked across her skin.

"Stand still. Do *not* squeeze your buttocks. If you do, it's going to get worse."

I proceed into several quick and hard whacks onto her skin, until she has to tense up and let out a huge, bellowing scream into the house, inspiring me to the far and distant opposite of mercy.

"To the mirror now," I say, "Hands on the dresser—feet together."

With Austria in anchor against the fine oak dresser, staring at her own tear stained face, I place the paddle again against the sorest, rawest place on her bottom. I raise the paddle and bring it down onto its target, making her cry out again in that same loud, strained voice. Without a word, I do this again… and again… and again, until she is sobbing like a wayward child, her voice in woman's siren begging me to stop. But there is no rest for the weary. I have raised a solemn bruise onto her right buttock. And now, I intend to beat her golden skin to blood.

Every whack on her naked, bruised bottom elicits a full yell into the house, making me wonder with delight, what if Susan comes to the front door and hears these delightful screams. I drive the paddle into her like a gold miner beneath the earth, chopping, pounding, hammering forward to the mother lode, that golden vein, the life's blood itself.

Several more times I paddle the same spot, now angry with momentum, using her screams and crying to justify what I must do here, the taming of this wild creature, her beating into submission.

"Unsqueeze your *ass*, I said!"

"Please no more," she says, "Sarah please no more. We've got Susan Marshall coming…"

"The bitch isn't here yet is she? *Is she!"*

Without another word, I continue the destruction of her normal skin, until both buttocks are beyond black and blue, and the rough skin is marred with angry white patches of burned flesh.

"Sarah, I love you, please help me understand."

Help you understand what, my dear! That this is the paddling I have held back from my girls for 20 years, for fear that they would tell it to their father? That my groin is on fire, from the sight of the bruises and obvious pain I have caused? That the sound of your screaming has become like wine to my spirit in craving?

"Just a few more," I say, which I admonish tirelessly, until I am satisfied that her skin has been cut, and there is indeed a spot of blood on the paddle.

I go over to her and turn her around to me—kissing every inch of her face. Especially the tears. Hugging her while she sobs and cries continuously.

Loving her.

In the aftermath of trauma, we sit quietly in the bedroom, both fully clothed, her in my lap in my cushioned chair. What was done, had to be done, to be sure—as violence tends to be the super glue of bonding; if violence enters therein, it breaches the ultimate barrier line, and if a relationship survives this forbidden undertaking, it becomes stronger than ever.

Though she has hardly said a word to me in the last hour, I know that every kiss to her cheek, every reassurance whispered in her ear brings her closer to where I know she has already come back to me. Our relationship has blossomed, I suppose, to a place so far beyond lust as to be tangible to us, and neither of us can imagine ever again being apart.

Chimes play the music of our heartstrings, to flow hopeful anticipation in the air around us. From the finger of a woman I've known, pressed upon the chimes of our present life—I hear the song of the visitor, to play the modern key for what once was, when all were alerted by a knocking at the door. Yes, there is always so much to fear... from a fateful knocking at the door. This knocking is the ringing of the hidden chime, played so beautifully in Mozart's eternal key, a calling upon the Sonata Facile in C. *God that's beautiful,* Austria says, concerning the doorbell of her dreams, the answer of her dreams come calling. But *this is not a dream,* I tell her, *this is it... and this is real.* I tell Austria Goldman to "go get your Destiny" at the door, adding "if you can still walk," gently patting her bottom in the shapely new jeans and black turtleneck cashmere, to put every curve fully on display, while hiding the blood and bruises underneath.

In painful reconciliation, in the acceptance of her calling, Austria Lee Goldman, daughter of Laura Ingrid Stone, granddaughter of Helen Ingrid Komar, glides down the grand staircase in upper class splendor, bankrolled by a billionaire's wife. In full, sore hip switching confidence, the half happy, half white beauty opens the big front door, that climbs up to windows wherein only the angels will ever see.

The two of them exchange wary glances, amidst the *hi's* and high-classed *fungalooga* smiles and phony, passive aggressively polite laughter. One laughs in truth, the other, in desperate longing for it.

The yellow-pretty reaches her hand out to the shapely, sophisticated yellow blonde, pulling her into this lap of luxury, to walk slowly in back breaking, talkative tension built up from the years of desperation, and the weeks of its newfound acquaintance. These desperate housewives are married to ambition, to the reason of Destiny, which overrides their indecision, beholden to their sister in law Fate, as she guides each placid step towards the end of the rainbow.

But Delusion circles the sun in a band of color, that shines through the haze upon every best laid plan.

"What?"

At the table in our kitchen, sheltered from a new mist of rain, the lovely woman stares at the older, more sophisticated lovely woman, on the edge of a rolling, roaring sea.

"I know it's hard to accept, Honey. There are so many places with such good writing, and I must say there is plenty of drama, which you do well. But I just don't see the kind of sales potential that we would need to justify spending the thousands of dollars we would need to spend through editing, printing, let alone marketing—the cost would just be too high to warrant a book that would barely sell enough to cover even part of its own expense."

Beautiful, unbelieving lips are borne bountifully apart, to complete an expression of such profound, lucid shock as to defy description. The stunned, catatonic look sparks an energy in the Marshall soul, to inspire her to the same condescension, the same patronization, the same passive aggressive indignation Austria has felt blasting her since childhood.

"Can I be honest with you... Austria? I've seen it a hundred times. I was a literary agent for over ten years, so I know where you're coming from. All writers understand that same desperation you feel—believing they've written a bestseller that will *'change the publishing industry as we know it'* and that will impact our society like the nothing since *The Lovely Bones* and *Bastard Out of Carolina*. I mean, you put your whole being, every part of yourself—months and years of writing into that first book— you've suffered and cried over it—heck you gave birth to it. It's like a child of your own body. But more often than not, Honey, that first novel is nothing but a catharsis for something that happened in our real lives. It's our 'test pancake' if you will, and because of that, will probably never get published."

Test Pancake?

"It's one of the harshest realities a writer has to face, Austria... and by the way that is a lovely name—"

"Thank you."

It is my lady's last ditch effort. The leaping forward to catch the moving train, the hopeless grasping at straws that have been blown apart from stability, and threaten to vanish forever.

"There's a lot of bad agents out there that are just in it for the money, Sweetie—if they don't see dollar signs they're not interested. If they take a novel like yours that they know is not quite ready, it's because they're in the business of 'flipping' these books for a small profit to editors they have a prior agreement with. Books that usually spell the end of a writer's career before it even gets started. But mostly they just reject and reject these poor writers without telling them why and it's Hell for you guys, I know, but the truth is that *perseverance* can only get you so far in this business. And writing new books won't help, because the same mistakes that got them rejected before will get you rejected again and again. Without *enlightened* perseverance, you'll never be published."

"Couldn't we... couldn't we just edit... or do rewrites... or...? It's been so many years."

Susan Marshall takes the requisite deep breath, her hands clasped on the table. She looks down at those selfsame, lying hands, according to the author across from her. Hands white with the privilege of denial.

"No amount of editing can fix what is inherently unpublishable. It's a good story, it really is, but not for big budget, mainstream publishing."

"You just mentioned *Bastard Out of Carolina,* didn't you? That entire book revolves around..."

As it is with a person in a dying airplane, Austria accepts the calming medication from her brain, and its mixture with the simmering, repressed emotion underneath.

"That book is probably the single exception to this rule. But I know as well as I know my own body—abuse books don't sell. And *nobody* in the publishing industry wants them. Your book is too depressing and down market—no legitimate publisher in the world will ever be interested. The foolishness of sending this same novel to agents and editors, over and over again under different names, different titles, is surely a waste of your time and mine."

The sorrow—the unspoken defeat—the devastation in Austria's expression causes Susan to have to close her legs tighter under the table, and adjust herself in her chair.

"Why don't you spend time writing something new instead of spending months and years submitting this same book to agents and editors who just keep politely declining? They can do that forever… it's their job to reject manuscripts and authors they can't sell. You need to write something new that is completely unrelated to abuse. Put this book away for at least a year. I would even consider getting *therapy*—if this is the product of something that really happened."

Austria stares blankly at her dead body of a manuscript. Hardly able to look cultured civility in the eye.

Susan Marshall stands up from the table, in full gray business attire, skirt fit snug to hips on the broad side of 48 years and counting.

"I can't believe it. You made me wait, made me suffer for six weeks…"

"What?"

A pause…

"Bitch, you heard me."

Susan Marshall tucks her lips—to stifle something that might have been a laugh—then breathes a deeply smug, self assured breath of inner confirmation, that every expectation from birth to death was just made plain.

"Miss Goldman, I almost sent my assistant over here. I don't have time to spend—time to *waste* talking to angry, depressed writers who don't really want to be helped, but just want to be published—in spite of the fact that what they've written has not a chance in Hell of being published."

"Yet if you liked it, if your *daughter* had written it the damned thing would probably be going into print by now."

"It's not even a question of liking, Honey, in the book business it's not who you know but what you write. And like with any other art form, if it's worth anything, somebody will find it. Your attitude tells me that you're not prepared for this business anyway. I came over here as a favor, to reach out to you with some very valuable insight to help you get published someday, and now you're calling me a bitch?"

"What the fuck else would you call somebody who just treated people the way you did? You practically *promised* Sarah that this was for real. Why the Hell didn't you just call us six weeks ago?"

"I don't know where you came from or how you tricked Sarah into trying to help you, but you are clearly not ready to be a published writer, no matter what you believe. You have not put in the work you need to even *think* about being published."

"I have worked my ass off for ten years, Miss, learning more about writing than you ever even thought you knew! You could not begin to know how many times that book was rewritten…"

"Look…I don't have time for this. Good luck to you , Ms. Goldman. I'm sure that someday you might get lucky if you keep going, but frankly I don't see it happening… I've got to go, I can see myself out—tell Sarah I'm sorry it didn't work out…"

"What gives you the right! What gives you the right to just walk in here and shit on my life and walk out like a goddamn Queen?"

In the same, frustrated sigh that so many defense lawyers have breathed walking away from an angry, hopelessly incarcerated prisoner, she turns on the melody of *"Miss Goldman get some help"* and walks away, wide hips swinging back and forth like a watch on a chain, to hypnotize the unlucky onlooker.

From somewhere within, whispered from a past unbeknownst—there is a warrior's strength of boldness, the involuntary motion of aggression, which powers her legs forward until she catches the woman in mid stride in the big, plush living room, grabbing her hard by the arm and swinging her around.

"Take your hands off me. .. you crazy *nut*."

"Not until you tell me the truth—why won't you help me?"

"I *can't* help you! Your book won't sell, we *can't* publish it! What do you want me to do—you can't get a book published just because you know somebody."

Susan Marshall's own strength compels, and she wrenches her arm from the Austrian grip.

"That's not what you told Sarah, you told her it's *who* you know."

"Yes, and the 'who you know' had better like the manuscript or it is dead. And nobody in our office can stand your book, Miss Goldman. They didn't even want to *read* it when they found out what it was about."

"Can you even *tell* me what the book is about? Did you even read it yourself?"

"I read it alright—and I knew from the first chapter I wasn't going to publish it."

In the mist of November rain outside, Lee hears a phantom roll of thunder, reverberating across the landscape of herself, the wildness of who she has become. This phantom thunder rolls throughout the misty regions, though perhaps in the mind of insanity alone, as there is no thunder in a November rain.

"That's right. We don't publish big budget porn. Which until you learn how to write that's all you're ever going to produce. Truth is, I remember you from two years ago, when you sent your book to my agency. The Susan Marshall Agency. When you tried to call it "In the Midst of Paradise," then "The Lonely," then "A Portrait in Gray", then I think you tried to call it… "Emily" or "The Angry Blackbird" or something…"

Austria's eyes widen. Shock relaxes both lips again.

"Call of an Angry Blackbird," she says. Pitifully.

"What*ever*. Baby, you've been blacklisted for two years anyway," she says, her face bold and bitter now, "and no matter what you do, that book will never be published. Your book is not literature. It is *trash*. A farce of unpublishable *junk*. And nobody wants to read some boring, silly story about an abused girl that grows up and *fucks* her mother…"

From the evening tides, crashing the shores of Devastation, the power rides—to where the arm and hand of Austria Goldman flies in motion, and the quick, hard slap knocks Susan Marshall nearly off her feet.

"Not only," she breathes, holding her face, "will that garbage never be published… but you're going to jail. You have no talent. And your book is an unlikeable, unwanted piece of *shit.*"

Austria feels the divining warmth, as it starts at the top of her head, burning her sinuses and downward to her legs and groin. Through the fog of rage, moving adrift as a spirit, the Austria Entity glides to the Susan Force, gripping her arm around her throat from behind. The woman can only grab Austria's arm, which is locked in place—her pretty, middle aged face already puffed and reddish from the ordeal. Like a woman in familiar terrain, my love takes Susan down to the ground holding on while the woman kicks and tries to cough. The commotion carries through the house just enough to make me open the bedroom door and wander slowly down the hall. Emerging from around the corner, the scene plays through the railings on the staircase and the upstairs banister—the scene of two beautiful women locked in violence. To my horror, I see Austria on her back, with the 48 year old, sophisticated Susan Marshall pulled back against her, Austria's legs around the woman's body and her arm around her choking throat.

I run down the stairs quickly, screaming Austria's name, punctuated by the chord of '*please.*'

"Hold this bitch's legs…"

"Austria, let her go!"

"I said hold this bitch's legs goddamnit now *do it!*

Controlled by something other than judgment or reason, I grab Sarah Marshall's legs and wrap them together as one, feeling her hopeless endeavor to kick, listening to her choke and strain to take a single breath. And suddenly, with my heart, I want to move up her body so I can lay full on top of it, my face close to hers—so I can watch the light go out in her bulging eyes.

What songs they sing in Jubilee—
Underneath the Cherry Orchard Tree
The Voice of God is Destiny—
In the misty rainfall by the sea

"Close the bitch's eyes," she says, as I obey the voice of my young mistress, closing Susan Marshall's eyes unto death. I want to give the sleeping woman mouth to mouth and take her to the emergency room and tell them we found her on my property. But as we both rest uneasy, the only sounds being our breathing, and the phantom whisper of rainfall, I know as surely as sundown, that I have never seen such a disgusting barrel of fish as what lives and dies in her profession.

"I take it that you heard. You heard what she said."

"I heard her say your book was trash. Then I saw…"

Unbelieving, refusing to receive—I stare down at the lovely older woman—so beautiful, even so sophisticated in death.

"Is she really dead?" I say. "Is this a dream?"

It's a nightmare, Mary, now bury this merry scheme! These words echo this landscape of new reality—this alternate truth my life has grown. In the other world, the one I long for, Austria graciously accepts Susan Marshall's unkind refusal, then escorts her through their same passive aggressive smiling to the door—then she finds me in the upper room, then sinks to her knees in front of me, and I spend the afternoon consoling her sobs and weeping incapacity. Then we get up and find the nicest restaurant I can remember, where we would dine and dismiss all our cares away.

"We'll bury the bitch here," she says. "On the outer edges of your property."

While buried in sickening fear, I hear the words *"on the outer edges of your property"*... and my mind finishes it—*'in the nighttime forest wood.'* I start there, gazing at the exotic young woman underneath the sexy, wide hipped older woman, still holding on tight, still dealing with the consequences of her actions, the arrival of the black funnel cloud, and the irreparable devastation it causes.

I don't touch her. I don't lay down the ridiculous, requisite line *'what are we going to do?'* Nor the self righteous, self indulgent flight of moral superiority and take charge judgmentalism. No, I don't say 'look at what you've done' or 'you need to get up from there' or 'you need to turn yourself in.' No. There is no easy and righteous solution, where we hold hands in a courtroom while she is being pulled away by the attending officers, nor will there be our loving arms by whispers over prison phone visiting hours. No. There is no easy solution to our problem, and no easy path to freedom or peace of mind.

This November wind howls our undoing, in the thick evergreen woods behind our property. We have not been aware for quite some time as much as we are this moment, that our bodies are what the scriptures refer to as "the weaker sex," for our arms are on fire with this labour. First the trash bags and duct tape, and the trunk of my appropriately black Mercedes. Then a hauling of shovels, a pick axe, and this empty shell across the vast lawn field of grass to the woods, then a dragging of Susan Marshall beyond the border inside.

The air is strong with the smell of wet pine. The sweet pungency of our misdeed. We chop, chop, chop hard into Northeastern woodland soil, cutting the ground without mercy, to lay abomination within. Then we dig, dig, dig our way downward, deeper than feeble Mediocrity, down to where secrets lay; where problems are laid to take root, and grow back through the soil as ghostly truth resurrected.

Sheltered from the autumn mist by the trees, in a rolling gray twilight, she stands suspended in the rectangular crevasse, where the glacier of our world is split in two—standing in the hole dug in the pine forest floor. Standing still now, to her waist inside, not another shovelful of earth forthcoming. She tosses the shovel out, a darkly hooded silhouette at sundown, whose hand I reach out to in the approaching evening day— which shall remain hidden behind these clouds of grieving.

I reach out to her, and pull her up from the grave. Together, we lift the thing bound and taped in black trash bags, to unceremoniously, hatefully swing it through the air where it flies, in slow motion, slamming into the mound of dirt on the other side of insanity, sliding down, rolling down the loose, wet dirt—falling to the bottom of the grave.

"I hope the bitch wakes up," she says, spitting inside, all of which my brain very nearly leaves unprocessed. Somewhere in the slow motion bewilderment of it all, I see the silhouetted figure hand me the shovel, and beautiful lips motion in sound I don't really hear, but still fully perceive. I strike the first loose pile of earth with pure trepidation, through unequivocal longing for clarity. Pulling, sliding, spooning the dirt down on top of the taped trash bag figure down below. Did it move? Did it flinch? Did it scream? No. The scream is coming from inside my own mind.

I turn to look at the car, noticing that Lee is inside, but not screaming as I had thought. What I hear is the cello of Ofra Harnoy as it begs Paul McCartney's question, concerning the passing of the years, and the sixty fourth candle at the Isle of Wight. From the speakers inside the car, my mind is set adrift while I move the dirt as quickly as I can. *You do half and I'll do the rest*, I remember her saying now, to strains of my own desperation still sung by the cello. Yes, I too know that what I feel for Austria is forever, And I Love Her.

As I feel her falling in the misty gray, I fill the newly dug hole with earth, to the bygone hopes of Yesterday, and every shattered dream of tomorrow. In the power of yesterday, I no longer believe. And yes, there is a shadow over me, to darken the coming days. This thing that I do, I have to do, as it is with the rest of humanity, as the end of the world is foretold by human behavior, and the shameful things we do in secret. In the way she moves, in the way this woman has wooed me astray, there is Something; something so powerful that it has gathered me up into the clouds, to whirl and shake me into freezing, then downward in a spiral— back to the crashing, sounding sea.

There is an evil spirit around domestic violence. It is unequivocally from the Devil. When the wrong thing is said to the wrong person at the wrong time, it is to stand at the mouth of the Dragon's Lair, and scream and shriek for his attention. It is to wake up the sleeping dragon, who shakes his head, and remembers that he breathes fire in the dead of night. And whosoever shall be unfortunate enough to stand nearby will be cooked out of this world into the next one. These blue and black flames were awakened in my house, and I saw a family and career woman lose her life because of it. And I stood by and did nothing. Does that make me as completely to blame as she—as the beautiful dragon that burned the woman in fire?

In the twilight falling, by the body buried underneath the pine, by the cello that sings of God's love to a dying world, we sit in fine, Mercedes luxury—both filthy with exhaustion, breathing a sigh that what we have done, we did quickly.

"Her car is out front."

"I know," she says. "I took the keys before I wrapped her up. Everything else is in the ground."

"Austria… I'm sorry to have to ask… but… what were you *thinking?* On second thought, God, what was *I* thinking? Never mind. Because I held her down while you finished… choking her. And then I helped you bury her. I don't have the right to judge you and ask you stupid questions about anything. I don't have the…"

Whatever words were there are choked as completely as our victim, their feeble lives sucked to another part of my brain.

"I was thinking about Ingrid."

"Who?"

"My mother. Laura Ingrid. And how she had trained me for this without knowing it. To snap like a dry twig. And now I'm thrown in. Inside a blazing hot furnace."

"Are you going to turn yourself in?" I ask defeatedly, "and show them the body? Then say that I wasn't at home when you did it?"

"Is that what you want?"

Unbeknownst to me, my spirit resists all twinges of remorse, even regret, and there is a part of me that is glad we did it.

"Well… we can't leave her car here."

She pulls the keys from her sweatshirt pocket, tingling them like a tiny bell chime.

It is written, that Fate decides over Reason. This is surely the case for us on this long, dark road, far south of New Bethlehem, somewhere east of the Appalachian Mountains. I had remembered one brief flash of a connection I had achieved with Susan Marshall over a year ago last summer, when she had said to me *"I ought to just go home to Charleston. My Momma's got a big house down there and she keeps beggin' me to come home. If I ever get smart and leave my husband…"*

While this vision plays in the air around me, the hills of West Virginia loom large and dark beneath a starry sky, below the grieving clouds from where we have come from. As if we know where we're going, I follow her as the blind leading the blind, towards nowhere, towards the edge of the earth itself. It seems as though we will drive off a dead end road over each and every horizon, and plunge into outer darkness, and the glory of the Second Heaven.

As we cruise west of the Alleghany mountains, a killing woman and her benefactor, I can feel no condemnation in my heart, nor fear of Divine Retribution for my new daughter in crime. For it is written somewhere in this vast and infinite starry night, that as surely as it is with the lovely woman and me, the buried woman's next comeuppance was also overdue.

Somewhere, in the darkest part of Charleston. Beige luxury is abandoned—in the heart of the West Virginia night. Somewhere west of the Alleghany Mountains, two women fade into black, the four wheels of their fervent flight. Black Mercedes luxury rolls the darken'd streets of this town, then past the Appalachian chain. Lost in blackness, in the void behind us, rises the mountains of West Virginia, across a fervent Autumn's night.

From the blackened outskirts of Charleston, through the loneliness that is nighttime Kanawha County, we cruise the dark and Wealthen Stream, grieving for the Land of Plenty. Across the time and the miles east again, we contemplate both sides of our creation. Of the empty, rolling sarcophagus we left behind—the stone coffin disguised in steel, the monument to capitalist greed, the ultimate moving symbol of wealth and gain. This empty steel coffin, abandoned to the far west of our world. Whilst therin lies the truth buried too deep to know, escaped east of the stretching Appalachian hand through rainy Pennsylvania, below the Catskills and onward—under the Connecticut skies of grieving.

The Cherry Orchard

Through the early morning mist, in the nighttime before dawn. Black Mercedes luxury rolls through the open gate. Down the asphalt path, and the sleeping branches of the Cherry Orchard trees in weeping.

From the wisp of an early morning dream, I awaken, my dream world corresponding to a rolling stop. With my eyes closed, they are wide open in another world, in one of the parallel earthly planes we see every night. I had dreamt of Austria and me plunging to our deaths from some gigantic bridge or another—I remember the scene had been very tranquil, almost peaceful, save for the otherworldly crash of concrete and metal, then our smooth flight toward the water below. She had let me sleep through the last part of our journey back home, having been subjected to the gray world all along; which brought a sky of black-gray clouds, with a towering black tornado whirling towards our wooden house of poverty.

From these signs I awaken—across the border from yesterday into tomorrow. As I gaze at my driver in half sleep, I can feel a life of false hope, empty promises and broken dreams come to dire fruition.

"Austria, did it really happen?"

"No," she says, in the wist of exhaustion along Melancholy Way. "It was all just a dream."

I would have been so inclined to believe her if not for the tired aching of every muscle, wherein the motion of digging is burned into, along with the burning soreness in both my hands, and the stench of pine still so strong in my nostrils. I close my eyes again, and I see a rolling gray cloud bank as wide as Creation itself, moving across a blue sky.

We walk together, Death and Hell. We walk together, the two of us, through the early morning rain. Undaunted. Uncaring. Unaccepting of what constitutes remorse. Unguilty. We walk together—twelve hours from the burial beneath the pines. Unrested. We walk together—unprotected from the morning mist, unjaded to the splendor of what we see. We step through the gigantic doors of this November, and coming nights of the Forest Moon. We walk together, the writer and I, into the lap of luxury, unconcerned now by what we have left behind, stopping together as if by instinct at the stairs.

We climb this weary stair case, the unwitting executioners, the agents of whatever evil that must come. This evil, arisen, borne from what lives in the hearts of women and men, by tragic predestination, preordained from before the world began. We walk together, the two of us. No longer cursed to push against a dark destiny. Unresisting. Accepting our life and calling. We go upstairs in the fine and grand, on the majestic current of living. Closer to her, I am, than any other person I have ever known. A person who refuses to make me feel less about myself. Less about who I am, or what I have done. A person of inner reverence and respect for life, though by Irony's Hand, she hath taken it by choking. Though she has buried it by blood. By the blood of raw and bruised skin upon her buttocks. Upon the blood and bruises of scars unhealed. Uncured by time or attrition. A woman of deep and abiding scars of agony, buried in the reserve of her soul and spirit. Quickened by the evil of cold betrayal. Activated by determined , deliberate condescension.

What evil must it have been, to have made this young woman do such a thing! What is the sum and total of unrighteous motivation! What is the boomerang effect, concerning Karma, and reaping of the choices sown! An eye for an eye, a tooth for a tooth, before the age of grace was born. A life for a life—still for those in battle forlorn. A life taken in self-defense of a sort, I see. By the hands of the nude warrior that stands before me in my room. Unashamed, as she stares at the beautiful scars that run across her golden skin, and of those that run black and bloody blue across her hips and thighs. Those that were put there by me, as I establish authority, by the power of the paddling wood.

In renewed fascination, untempered, unfettered by our flight from sleep, I go to the mirror where she stands, to study the power of perversion, of what is done in the name of discipline. Unmerciful. Unsympathetic to the new pain I know she feels, as the lady ranch hand with her knee in the calf's side on the ground, and the branding iron burning smoke by the howling of pain. I step up to her, still fully clothed, hugging the naked woman who is a little taller than me, so that my hands go around her tiny waist to her back, with the gentlest rubs to her branded hips and bottom. The most magnificent hips they are, amazingly wide across the buttocks, full and rounded besides. Wide set and substantial by birth alone, passed from both the African and the European branches of her family tree. A *million dollar ass*, to what some vulgar tendencies might arrive, if they could see what I see in the mirror, such a powerful and noticeable part of her when she is unclothed.

From her whispers, I am invited to where she must bathe. Where she must try and wash the filth away. The killing woman walks into the bathroom, into the water palace, now inspired to awe at the Amazonian perfection of what I see. And I turn to the woman in the mirror now, to watch her remove the uncompromising blouse, to reveal the gigantic bra underneath. The sound of the palace waterfall, to the shower noise in the bathroom, I shimmy away from the jeans, and the shoes and socks until my black underwear and bra are alone. Then I slip the bra straps down, then take the easy, unglamorous way out, lowering the bra away from the big boulders underneath, then turning the bra to the front and unlatching it.

I stand in front of the mirror. Unclothed. Staring a piercing, glowering gaze.

Unloving.

he next day barrels us both awake, somewhere well past the noon day. Both of us are still nude, half covered under the sheet, still on fire from what we have done. That fire has now gathered itself, into Austria's scarred and bruised body, with her rolled over on top of me, us both engaged in the deepest and noisiest hugging kiss possible, until soon her lower body finds its place, and she must cease our rough kissing, to position our spirits anew. Like two power wires joined, the nerves that expand themselves to raging have grown fully, pressed together with her groin locked onto mine, my legs spread open to receive this punishment. Her body tenses as she begins to grind this Lady Cock onto mine, to light both of us on blue and black fire. My eyes roll back to where I am lost, and she suddenly raises up onto her strong arms above me, prompting me to open my eyes again. The open lips, the wrinkled brow, the pain on her face is such sublime contrast to the golden breast hanging down, both nipples beckoning my mouth to suckling water. I raise up, quickly to obey this thirst so quick. Clamping puckered lips onto her nipples like a starving baby cow on a swollen udder, by which the shudder runs through her body. To utter her voice in breathlessness and stutter. Something to the sound of *'suck my titties Momma... sug my ditty...'* clumsily escapes her parted lips, as her sliding groin becomes a grinding, pushing harder into where my own violence is born. I take her breasts in my hands, holding then as two eyes, staring the nipples as if they could see who has awakened them. She looks at my gargantuan softees, the wobbling water bags of wibble, woggling off to the sides. She lowers her head to a nipple, pulling the bibbling, squibbling flesh upward so high and so hard, the anguish now doubled on her face as she sucks and pulls. She lets it go in the loud, sucking *pop* sound, watching it return to its wide, wobbling shape. I use my arms to prop them up just enough, so that they wiggle and wobble, jiggle and bobble in her face—whereas her own new staring has begun, into the Eyes of Wobble...

And her grinding is now a bumping, and full fledged humping of our swollen knobs together, as she glances at what she sees as the beauty of my face, and the gigantic wobble of my Waterford Tits. I lay on my back still, hands at her waist to anchor us, legs open and back, watching her stare at one of my breasts as through commanded by it, slamming herself full and hard into my groin, until every muscle in her body tenses beneath jiggling flesh, and she lunges forward to my shoulder, to rest on the wave of convulsions, and the bellowing voice of howling grief and pain. In a voice surely inherited from her mother, she fills the room with the sound of a branded she-calf, being burned into an altered state of mind and body.

"Hi, Susan... I'm just calling to say how sorrow we were we missed you yesterday, we were here waiting for the good news and you never showed. I hope everything's alright, and give me a call okay? Bye bye now."

Austria watches me close the little cell phone, which I use but still truly despise.

"That was smart," she says. "If they check her voicemail…"

"How long should we wait before we go to her office?"

"She went missing on Sunday morning… Monday, we'll go to … we'll go the bitch's office. Hell, maybe we'll even go visit her husband and kids. How many did you say she had?"

"Two daughters. And a mother in Charleston."

Our walk through the hallowed halls of publishing is like a trip though a mausoleum—a ghostly place of high aspirations and low human concern. A place where scruples are crushed under foot, and common decency is rationalized away, all under the guise of intelligent, business-minded goodwill. Confident of earned prestige, amidst the smell of new cloth, new books and old money. And though there be space enough for infinite attempts at book form, the space strives for a look of saturation, as though any young writer could only believe that every publishing space in the universe is filled, and no sane writer could ever expect to occupy these hallowed halls of learning. The sight of all the books is making me dizzy, and the smell of them is making me sick.

"Miss Waters?"

Austria Lee and I stand at the door of a cluttered space that might be called an office. A bare walled, bare assed excuse of an office. A glorified storage space for a big desk, and far too many books stacked against gray walls. Un-neatly.

"Excuse me, but do you know Susan Marshall?"

Elaine Waters allows her cheeky smile to die. Mid 40's attractive. Not a breast or hip in sight, under the loose blue pullover and matching sweater. Detroit Lions blue, actually. Bluebird blue. Quite Beautiful.

"She's our senior editor. And you are…"

"I don't know if Ms. Marshall told you about us or not, but we gave her a manuscript of ours to read about two months ago, and she called us last Sunday and said she was coming to my house."

"Oh, you're Peter Bishop's wife..."

I have always been fascinated by what that piece of information can do to a person. They immediately take on the Nine Fruits of the Spirit—love, joy, peace, longsuffering, gentleness, goodness, faith, meekness *and* temperance—whether they be heathen or no, they are suddenly as disarmed as if I had disrobed down to my gigantic tits.

"...so you're the notorious Austria Goldman."

"Yes, Maam," the beautiful woman says, shaking Elaine's hand. Awkwardly.

"We haven't heard from Susan in a week," Elaine says. "But we had pretty much settled the issue of the novel."

Austria and I are locked and bound by the same gratitude—thankfulness that we wear this gift of armor, the protection of foreknowledge. Were we not informed, we both would have felt the Fear of Death, and would be in a thousand pieces on this office floor. We listen to her pompous, self important spew—spraying disillusionment and despair over us like cold water on a dead fireplace log. This poor, dumb woman! Enjoy thy poison spray! Relish thy condescension! Thine patronizations galore!

"...but the good news is that your writing shows such promise, Honey. Just keep at it. I'm so sorry that Susan didn't tell you herself. Nobody's seen her, we don't know where she went."

Both of us hang our heads in relief, that our Days of Fungalooga smiles have come and gone—that there is no reason to go on pretending, that happiness has anything else to do with who we are.

"Oh… oh sweetie you don't need to cry."

Elaine Waters stands up, floating over to Austria like an angel of mercy, bent over with false compassion and passive aggressive sadism and satisfaction. My look of wonder is genuine, at the ease of flow Austria's quiet tears have taken.

Jonathan Lovejoy

Penelope

*M*ozart plays a melody. In the key of Eschatology. Close your eyes and you will see… magic ingenuity.

Penelope Bishop is the key. To my own eschatology.

Penelope Bishop rides the wave. The Thanksgiving wave that flows. That descends from bitter, gray November skies, moving over the cities, and the countryside like a spirit. A spirit of fear and sorrow—a reflection of loneliness born. Pressing down on every institution, filled to capacity, with every Autumn Fool in motion. A tragic notion of upward mobility they possess. False nobility of earthly achievement.

The Spirit of Thanksgiving compels them homeward. Rushing, in haste to escape the loneliness in gray. Even those who would be estranged, have family tensions assuaged, long enough to reunite. To escape the loneliness. The fear.

Penelope Bishop rides the wave. Home to where her family awaits. In the Spirit of Thanksgiving.

The drive past the line of cherry trees is welcome and familiar. Ridiculous Prius status, rolling in.

The statuesque blonde parks the silver ride and disembarks into her world, unable to fully appreciate the contrast from here to there. Twenty three years of blonde prettiness, up and down the halls at Columbia, up and down the streets of Manhattan. Gathered up by this holiday spirit—the first of my three daughters to arrive. Having earned her way in with the proper grades at Harvard University as an undergraduate, and the proper lineage as an applicant. Blessed with a head for numbers as it applies to high finance, destined for Wall Street Chaos. Among the vast majority of driven personalities, where therein lies an abundance of talent, and the absence of inspiration. Moving from the privileged hot pan, into the fire of achievement.

Penelope Bishop walks alone. Across the asphalt path of luxury, towards the grand, tall white double door, with the golden brass door handles. Not pressing the doorbell soft and glowing—testing her luck upon the golden handle itself. And in keeping with the rest of her life, luck sees a smooth unlatching, and the swinging open into the Hall of Luxury. The grand entrance space, reminiscent of her mother's Crystal Palace, every vase and statue fearlessly ceramic white or glass crystal in nature, in contrast to the light oak drawer chests and desk near the front door. Further away and to the right is the elegant staircase rising, the same light oak wood aglow on the railing leading to the floor of the upper room. And this is where her attention is nearly drawn, unsure of where the strange sounds are coming from. The sound of breathing, of private, forceful talking, and then the distinct noise of a single, spanking sound—a very loud echo of a hand smacking bare flesh, then a loud release of a scream, or rather a sharp *yelp* from the kitchen—a deep, woman's scream as from the soul of a woman in labour.

From whence forth thy mother's voice—dear Penelope, as the sound of such great travail! What is the counterpoint to her melody, the voice phrasing such sublime euphonism, in divine support of its mistress song and key! Where is your mother, Penelope, amidst the sound of her travail? Who is the woman, the owner of the other voice, deeper and more subtle, which breathes words that our mind cannot sustain? Did you hear those words, Penelope, coming from the strange woman that you see, as you step around the corner in the kitchen? Who, what… why is she? Where did they come from, these two people? Across the grand kitchen to your right, at the big kitchen sink, you see a yellow skinned woman of proportions you have not imagined, the J-lo jello of junk in the trunk desire—nude and naked from shoulders to shins, except for the black straps about her buttocks and thighs! Pushing, squeezing her ample hips forward against those of a white woman bent over at the sink, a white woman with your mother's voice, Penelope!

In a shock of fear unknown to you since the paddlings of your youth, you stand bold in the sight of devastation, like a lady hunter pointing her weapon at a charging lion, but having not the courage to fire. Not a single, dissonant noise can you make to disturb the music of what you see in your Mother's Kitchen, the music that rises from the East, burning blue and black fire. You endure one last gaze at the Amazon's curved waist and full, rounded hips squeeze tight forward again, to activate the sound of the white woman's voice in labour again.

You turn away. Pulling yourself away, the scarred image of the woman's back burned into your mind, her strong, scared backside an unwelcomed memory. You tip quietly, quietly as a low pump heeled mouse—the sound of your steps drowned out by the Witch's Aria, your mother's sublime shrieking from the consented anal raping.

To the tragic sounds of this unknown aria, you tip as quietly as you can, to the careful opening of the door, through the flash of breasts clamped at the nipple, and your hasty retreat to a place to hide in, thy ridiculous Prius status again.

*W*anton violence and immoralities play a part. But don't they? From the beginning of time until now, the course of our lives is often carried by what pain we have caused, and what sufferings we give pause to. Oh, what things we have seen—what things have we done—to run the gamut of sin? Can we truly sit in judgment of one another, for the sinful things that we do? No, there is no condemnation to them who are in Christ

Jesus, I suppose. Oh, but wherein does lie our true condemnation? There are lines that are approached on our daily walk with one another—these are the lines and boundaries. Boundaries to what we hold dear—the borders to our homeland—where hypocrisies rise and fall, where self righteousness ebbs and flows— where so-called indignation is born from judgmentalism over one another. We look for opportunities to show ourselves in a better light than our fellow men and women, and oh, woe unto them by which that opportunity is given! No matter how small, no matter how trite the infraction—we set upon it with a magnifying glass and a bullhorn, to announce to Heaven and Earth that we are better than them, and cannot abide what unrighteousness we have seen. It is the Delusion of Morality, the illusion of conscience we adhere to—though not even for righteousness sake. No, it is far and away towards the opposite—where *sadism* arises from the depth of us, from where it is programmed by the fall of Adam, and we must ease the pain of this desire, and use this new opportunity to cause suffering, through punishment from what these people have done. Only our blessed Lord and Savior, who preached that we should not judge, only he had no unrighteous axe to grind! But oh, by humanity, what solemn axes there be, by what night doth cause these sparks to fly!

Sitting here in Prius status. Sheltered from the Thanksgiving dreariness and cold, Penelope Bishop watches the first drops fall from the sky, to renew the aim and focus of the day—which is to weep for wanton immoralities, and for those who have perished by the sword. Every drop on her window splashes energy to her disbelief, until it is a crashing shower of bewilderment, her face red with unspoken humiliation—her expression clouded with revulsion. Did she really see a strange woman in her kitchen, standing nude behind her mother, wearing a strap-on dildo, pushing it into her naked mother's backside? *"Did I really see that?"* she says aloud—unable to block out the words flowing through. *Did I see a light-skinned woman fucking my mother up the ass in our kitchen?*

Her Prius is more of a refuge than ever now. Sheltering her from the rainfall, and from the reality inside her mansion home.

Penelope Bishop sits in hiding. Drowning in the Autumn rain.

What dreadful revelations drift down in the November mist? Those concerning the paddling years, and questions raised over and over again—why every infraction, every imperfection was dealt with so severely. Why did every punishment involve so much pain? Pain and humiliation—was there ever a paddling or a caning that did not involve her breasts exposed? Even her two younger sisters— one a junior at Dartmouth, the other a fat-bottomed freshman at Princeton? Did Penelope, 18 years old as she remembers—did she really understand why she was called into her mother's bedroom—five years ago as a senior in high school, to take her then 16 year old sister's pants and underwear down? *Why did Mom,* Penelope wonders—*why did Mom make Kimberly take off her shirt and then her bra?* Why was her mother already in her own bra when she called Penelope into the room? What purpose—what part of justice was served, to bruise a sixteen year old's bottom black and blue because of a C on a report card? Even after Kimberly had begun to sob in defeat after only the first whack—why did her mother say *"You might as well save it, Sugar.*

Penelope, Take my bra off, so I can finish this good—and hold her mouth so I don't have to hear that noise..." Penelope remembers the fear moving down to her own groin, and the way Kimberly's pathetic voice vibrated her hand, wet from tears running down her face.

Here today, her Prius windshield frosted, misted under a gray and grieving rain, this day slides down her driver's side window in weeping, as she remembers the dark spirit descended on her mother's face, staring intently at Kimberly's bottom while laying the paddling wood in place. Penelope closes her eyes, wincing as the memory flows through her body—still unsure by what shadow is brought such a thing into the hearts of women and men. It was Mom's Modus Operandi, her signature move, to wield the heavy wooden paddles on their naked bottoms—and Penelope remembers suddenly, with certainty, that the more clothes her mother took off, the more severe the paddling. And if her mother took the time to expose her gigantic tits, then the corresponding paddling, or caning, would be dealt accordingly. As many as three hundred whacks she has counted, even periods of rest along the way, until all confidence, all endurance has faded to bitter despondency, brief hopelessness, and utter despair. What fires are they that burn, to sear the flesh of an accursed few! And what other fire is it that burns, to sear those scars that cannot heal? These are the Blue Fires of Perversion, that feed the Black Flames of Violence risen, to cause such shameful, secret pain and suffering.

My daughter tucks her lips, amazed by the phantom itching on her skin. Wondering how many of her fellow students, how many high minded, high class survivors she knows; survivors of their mother's pervertedness, and their father's epic depravity? Part of her is reduced to a bundle of nerves, when she remembers the abortion I helped her through as a nineteen year old college freshman, and whether or not I know who the father was. Whether or not her father's siren voiced his eternal damnation into his daughter's ear; whether Peter Bishop shook and jerked himself to ruin on top of his naked daughter in a hotel across the ocean, Penelope is sure that I don't know. But unbeknownst to my feeble, fragile excuse of a fine, fair-haired daughter, I know everything in her world—I am the unknown omniscient—the undiscovered ubiquity of her waking dreams. Yes, you spoiled blonde bitch—I am the twisted reality, corrupting the pure hearted fantasy you concoct with such spoiled, rich girl aplomb! The woman who bore you is a money loving society whore, who cares as much about you as a flop-eared cocker spaniel! What energies there be, have moved you from her womb to mine, to bend me over with such divine hatred of thee! Yes, girl, I am the Woman in the Kitchen, though not at the sink observing a pile of dishes, but a vile and decadent vial of wishes! Burn this into your brain, my sweet and dearest daughter, the yellow skinned African woman of beauty, who hath violated your mother's sanity!

Penelope Annabelle—remember thy sister! In your shiny itty bit of a coffin on wheels, under the mist of Connecticut Rain! Where is thy sister now, dear daughter, a twenty one year old junior at Princeton? What is it that Kimberly told you I did to Sandra on her sixteenth birthday night, when she was late for her curfew? Did she tell you that when shapely Sandra, little shapely Brunette Sandra Bishop got home after midnight, two hours after her 10:00 curfew that I took her into the bedroom, and lectured her infinitum on the merits of absolute obedience? Did you listen closely, as Kim whispered to you over the phone what she witnessed, of Sandra stripped down topless and birthday blue jeans just purchased, with hanging, D cup breasts exposed? Wherefore art Sandra's darkened areola's my dear—so much darker than your own! Her young breasts hung so bulbous and beautiful; smaller reminiscences of my own! Ah, but you weren't there Penelope—to witness what Kimberly saw. When I taped Sandra's sixteen year old breasts tightly at the chest, so her hanging bells would rise! Beige packing tape around each one, to hold them up white and blue! And then I took the caning rod and striped them like peppermint while Kimberly stood behind her and pinned her arms! With the stocking shoved in her mouth and tied, her screams were absorbed on her birthday night, Dear Penelope—of this report, do you recall? Oh, how close to trembling my body came that night; her big, floppy breasts taped up, my thin cane striping them to red, her rough screams absorbed into my stocking cloth. Thank God, dear Penelope, that you were not here in those last years, when the fire blazed azure tinted pitch in me!

Oh, yes, Penelope, this is your mother! These are your foundling sisters! Behind the closed doors of this mansion—these things we surely have done! But to our credit, to our benefit and protection, dear girl, no one could believe us if we told! Their passive- aggressive hypocrisy would rise as a concrete barrier, to protect them from the truth they could not bear! Sit still in the rain, my darling, lost in the Heart of Memory, your blood now cold with revelation. You are even afraid to turn the switch of your car— for fear we might hear! And who is *we*, Dear Penelope—who hath stolen thy mother's sanity! Yes, thank Jesus, my girl, that you were not here those nights, when the depressive spirits sought refuge in my body! When I fantasized myself to sleep night after night with dreams of Kimberly's and Sandra's fervent pain. When their pain became my pleasure—my treasured reason to live! Thank Jesus, Dear Penelope, that you had escaped to Harvard's Hallowed Halls!

And what of the golden yellow bodied beauty—the one who breaches my sanity? Ours is a bond beyond understanding of the mind. From the beginning of our time, I have felt joined with her, at one with the cause of her life; to merely be free of the burdens that weigh her down, the invisible weight that presses the air from her lungs to breathe. To learn how to endure the raging fires within, to walk the earthly plane as one—to ease the suffering of brutal memories, and of souls that burn in blue and black fire.

*A*fter the passing of an hour, in the rising torrent of rain and cold, Penelope emerges from the depth of the Sounding Sea, the sea of ashen gray regret. She steps again out of Prius status, the silver requisite ride, this time draped in a long gray travel coat, and a lovely gray umbrella to match. A fearful, wincing glance at the front door she can hardly imagine going through—then a long and wistful, yes, a *wistful* gaze across the lawn still so green in the Autumn gray. The cherry orchard trees stretch out a long, lonely path in the distance, trees so typically uninviting in the fall, under the November Forest Moon. Somewhere above these clouds of grieving, there is the daytime Moon unawares, unnoticed, unaffected by the sufferings of women and men. Under these same clouds of weeping, by the hiding daytime Forest Moon, Penelope Bishop wields her gray coat and matching umbrella, at the door she herself locked an hour ago, pressing the chime of Mozart evening song.

She waits patiently in the rain, uncaring, unconcerned of how long it takes me to get to the door—or even whether I will come to her at all. She waits in the Autumn rainfall, trying not to imagine what is keeping her mother, what is keeping me from a quicker trip through the mansion—to rescue her from the wet, weeping world.

The door swings open, and that right soon, to the mother-daughter of hers and mine—both either glad, or un-glad to be seen. My oldest daughter, my oldest stepdaughter—the billionaire's daughter—steps with me over the requisite carpet of greeting, the white petals of holiday good will, commenting, complimenting on the sights, sounds and smells of home—of holiday cooking wafting in from the kitchen. What of her strangely bewildered tone, as though she studies me, to see whether or not I am the mirror image—escaped from the parallel world closest by?

Through every pleasantry, some of them genuine, we walk through me gliding her slowly *away* from the kitchen, where another woman is now fully clothed, and helping me with our pre-Thanksgiving feast.

"Is somebody in the kitchen?"

"Ummm… as a matter of fact, there is."

"Well, who is it? I don't want to be rude— "

"Uh… let's get you settled in first."

"Mom, I know where my room is. I want to meet your guest."

"Penny, you don't just barge in and meet people. Go on up to your room and get settled in first. Did you pack a suitcase?"

Halfway up the plush, carpeted stair case, she seems distracted, transfixed upon by the spirits that had been eyeing us through the whited railing. She turns to engage the souls of antiquity, in the black and white, ancestral photos decorating the walls, as if she had never really seen them before, in particular the one of a sad, somber portrait of a heavy breasted woman from the early part of last century, circa 1919. Not my mother, nor my grandmother, but my own great grandmother Elizabeth Carol Brandonwood, a woman of poverty, I've been told, who made it a point that she would leave one thing in life worth leaving behind—this photograph dated in June of 1919, to send nearly one hundred years into the future. This photograph we step so gingerly by, appearing as a woman of means—breasts at the piano, too large for her body in the full length, full sleeved and up to the neck white dress—her first name passed all the way down to Sarah Elizabeth, who escorts her stepdaughter so gently, so gingerly bye and bye.

Oh, what sins flow the motherline! Like a raging river crashing along in devastation, and drowning of every unsuspecting soul! Oh, what spirits are we held prisoner by, she wonders, when we take the last step to the upper hall, where the gigantic photograph of myself now hangs looming, me in the seated position, at the same spirit piano I never learned to play, white bloused in a world with no color, my own bosom in full, mountainous view in the white cloth, also too heavy for my figure. For eternity, men and women will see this photograph, and wonder how such a bosom can come to be naturally, and what manner of unclothed appearance it can possibly be.

I guide the young soul past the Women of Antiquity, down the hall, and through the doors of her upper room.

"I'll be down in a few minutes," she says. "Can't wait to meet our guest."

I try as hard as I can to shrug off what I sense in her tone, smiling a little, closing her door. But there is a quiet confidence in her now that is unfamiliar—not quite the same young woman I am used too—the one that walks on pins and needles, needles and pins around me. Where is the bravery, from whence does it come? I'm sure I do not know—nor can I really care, as I hurry down the stairs, unrepentant, towards the unsuspecting guest in the kitchen.

The world spins a moment of time, plunging so many over the sheer cliffs of reason. Not ten minutes go by, before the lumps are in both Austria's throat and mine. Listening to the quiet clip clop, of heels as black as the heart of a killer. Quiet clip clopping away those heels, from the foot of the staircase, across the hardwood part of the living room floor, silent through the carpeted white and crystal palace room, then as a spirit adrift around the corner of our grand and spacious kitchen.

Penelope endures the shock wave of emotion. A literal cocktail of feeling from the neck spine to her lower back and groin, cold and painful to endure—but which dispatches heat into her blood. The woman who fucked Penelope's mother is here, in a white t-shirt and jeans. Eyes as green as jade—but still reflecting the sky above the Caribbean.

What humility encompasses me? What humiliation? My lover and my daughter—embrace!

"Penelope, right?" are the first notes in this Fungalooga Overture—followed by rising, noisy chords of nervous and fearful laughter. *"You can call me Penny"* strains out on winds alone—followed so closely by the preordained *"Hi, Penny,"* then the pretty bases sing their remarkable laughter again, as high pitched as they know how, to command the other instruments to awe. And then I hear the awkward pause, I see the amazement in my daughter's eyes, staring down the woman who fucked her mother, at a loss for what to say, or what to feel. But this grand opening continues on—as if they are old college sweethearts—back and forth until finally, the winds breathe *Aus - tri - a* in response to *"What's your name..."*

Then the happy main theme commences—a firm and gleeful handshake, a smiling and bumbling trip back to *"nice to meet you... again"* uplifted in the sprightly strings of laughter. I can only stand by, pretending to be minding the stove, though the mashed potatoes have already been made, and are ready to help the Martha Stewart tragedy in the oven.

"*Bah Bah, Black Sheep*
Have you any wool?
Yes sir, Yes sir
Three bags full

One for my Master
One for my Dane
One for the little girl
Who lives down the lane"

"I don't mind the whippings anymore. I guess when you're born and raised on something, be it pleasure or pain—you become accustomed to it, like the famous frog who swims in the pot until he boils alive, not even bothering to hop out and save himself. Eva Watson makes no pretense behind the walls of our suburban home. I sit in front of the TV or my computer, or lull around in the kitchen in quiet anticipation now, whenever she is at home. Waiting for her to call me to her bedroom in the twilight glow—to show me the psychology of sadism.

This is the beautiful church woman who smiled and clapped at me just this month, when I graduated from high school in Chapel Hill.

When she had approached me and my friends, my back had begun to itch from the nude strapping I had just endured the night before. But I don't mind the whippings anymore— being the most normal part of who I am—the most pedestrian part of my private life. You learn to endure pain after a while, until you finally convince yourself that it doesn't even hurt anymore. Yes. I don't mind the whippings. But the feel of the paddling wood on my skin—the wooden spoon upon my breasts—the fiberglass cane on the backs of my thighs— these have often left me at odds with brief sanity, leaving me trembling with pain and fear. Unable to stand still, unable to endure the fire. There are scars and bruises from my shoulders to my ankles. Old scars, new scars— bruises that never seem to heal. My face now bears one of these selfsame bruises from graduation night—still under my eye—the only difference now being it doesn't hurt anymore. Though I had been beaten so many times before—there was a ferocity to this one. An animal energy that I had not felt before— perhaps activated by my new found freedom— being a high school graduate and all. And when it was over, as I sat on the edge of her bed— both of us fully clothed this time, she actually spoke the words—*"And don't think I'm going to let you out of my sight. You're staying in this house until I tell you that you can leave. You'll go to college when I say you can go to college—you'll get a job when I say you can get a job. And as far as men and marriage goes you can forget it, because I'm your man and you are married. Did you hear me?"*

Among the swirl of images, amidst the sights and sounds of voices—teachers, friends, mother and me, is the sound of our noisy breathing—her behind me bare skinned—naked from top to bottom as am I, her hands under my arms and clasped about my neck in a Full Nelson hold. I am bent over from the pressure and the weight of it—being pushed around the bedroom like a piece of furniture—being wrestled into submission by Eva Dove. Eva Watson. Statuesque—strong, beautiful. And every so often, my body is rocked by a hard thrust of her groin to my buttocks—to remind me that this punishment is perversion, and her perversion is pleasure. I'm always in some kind of wrestling hold or another, until my fervent discomfort is achieved—and her forlorn comfort is acquired. And the tragedy, I suppose, is that I can understand the pounding, though it is still humiliation—that it sends a wave of pleasure to my groin every time it happens. Does she know? Does Eva know that in secret—as she holds me bent over by the back of my neck as she pounds hard into me with her strong, white body, does she know that my breathing is to release the energy of the light and fleeting orgasm she has caused?

Sometimes I wonder if I am not adopted, or was found abandoned somewhere rather than created, birthed, and brought home from the hospital by this woman. I had heard about molestation, incest, even imagined about it myself, as all hearts are capable of such vulgarity. It's a sign of the end times, I think, that these secrets are going to be uncovered. But it's still very hard to accept sometimes that Eva Dove, Eva Watson is my mother, and the things I had only heard about and imagined have been happening to me since I was a child. As I lay pushed face down onto the bed, still gripped in the behind the neck wrestling hold, amazed by the strength of the pushing, listening to her hot breath in my ear—I know that I have endured something paramount to a raping, and yes, Eva Watson is my birth mother..."

At her desk, in the gray of the upper room, Penelope pours over the pages of a dead life. Sickened. Disturbed. Disgusted. Disillusioned. In disbelief that this woman is even in the *world*, let alone in this *house*. Austria Goldman? *Who the Hell is she.. what is she? Is she half Latino or something—what the Hell color is she, anyway? Mom hired her to be the maid and the cook and to run errands and help her manage the house— yeah, right. She wandered onto this property like a stray dog, and Mother took one look at those big, sad eyes and big, soft lips and went Lady Gaga over her, yes, and that being apt enough, as Mother too has nearly lost her mind with grief...*

But what grief? The sadness of being a brunette beauty with dark eyes and a strong, almost European sensuality in her features? The misery of carrying around breasts heavy enough to give a goddess envy, and to incite lust and fear in man, woman or child? Is it the pain of being the Mother-come-lately to five attractive well mannered, college educated children, all who keep pressing for her approval even in adulthood? Is it the sorrow of being the wife of a billionaire, though absentee, who still has many kind gestures and words of hopeful and future fidelity? What epic loneliness must it have been, Dear Mother, to make you drag this pretty bum in off the street, and pay her to keep you company, to make her believe that this depressing excuse of a pornographic whatever she has written ever had a snowball's chance? Did you tell her, Mother, that you could help her simply because you were attracted to her? I will most likely finish reading this thing you have given me to see, by rights of explanation and discovery—so I can find out who this woman is, and why I had to sneak away from the kitchen earlier today, because I saw her naked and strapped, pushing it so deep into the back of you. Yes, I well read, Mother, to learn what perversion is, and of what part of it thou hast taken.

Penelope! Read until your eyes bleed! Until your soul screams in terror! Until your body is so racked with lust you will have to disrobe! Cry out for Redemption, Dear Penelope—thou cannot cease from sin! Go to the wind and rain of thy balcony—overlook the Back Lawn of Beauty! How are you indeed devastated, my dear, to discover something so deep and dark about your mother—so much more unspeakable than even what you have already known! Look to the distant woods, Penelope my dear! Feel the calling from within! Contemplate the solemn images that have tormented these business school nights, when you see the cherry trees and the woods of your mother's property—burning blue and black with fire!

Memories coalesce in the winter wind, moving across January skies of gray. Every thought, every action, every event of mankind is drawn into these clouds of gloom, where they are frozen in time, made heavy in the storm of regret, until they drift across a landscape of cold and winter white. Memories of phone calls and questions ad nauseam, investigations and lies come and gone, all adrift now helplessly over our mansion estate, and the massive field of snow. We drift the long path under the cherry orchard trees, all of them frozen asleep under the winter Mountain Moon. It seems that every branch is covered in old and new fallen snow, heavy laden with every kind of memory and regret. Somewhere in the infinity of snowfall, the evil we have done hath coalesced, and fallen to the earth in winter grieving. We had searched our hearts through the arrival of Thanksgiving, and the suspicious looks from my sons and daughters at the table, especially from Penelope, about who this beautiful woman was, this beautiful loser who was supposed to be some kind of a writer or something, who now is their mother's (stepmother's) live-in maid and personal assistant.

Peter and Paul did not hide the requisite obliging, the good-natured and empty threats of grabbing Austria and biting her on the neck like a couple of vampires, neither of them quite used to women of such purely white and exotic beauty both all at once, with J-Lo Jello besides. Oh, what it must have done to their poor cocks and balls to have endured even a day in this house with that woman, with no chance of ever seeing her do the Hawaiian hips and belly dance slip, with her golden skin, rounded D cups pushed up, and a waist curve hardly imagined and never seen. Though they did the best they could not to act like J.D. and his brother from *Scrubs*, I know their groins were both burning as hot as a fireplace poker in Sarah Palin's livingroom. And though young Kimberly and young Sandra, (whose butt is likened unto Austria Lee's) were both reserved and even quietly suspicious, I could tell that they were both powerless against the natural charisma, the charm that exudes from physical beauty alone, when it is coupled with a genuine humbleness and meekness of the spirit. My poor Austria's attempt to cope was heartbreaking—and I think I was a little surprised by the realization, that despite her obvious talent and appearance, being a novelist who was seriously prettier than all of us put together, her manner was one who fought to conceal an extremely shy, sensitive nature. Especially at Christmastime, when old Peter Jack himself ruled the roost (he had spent Thanksgiving with his mistress in Dubai). Austria had relaxed into the sweetness of a well paid domestic—cleaning up after everyone constantly, until Peter finally scolded her and made her sit and watch a stupid game of charades with two other couples and me. Memories of that night—Christmas night—send a shiver up my spine. I remember feeling too, the presence of Divine Luck, as luck has no morality, protecting Austria and me from the ghost of Susan Marshall, who lurks our property even as I think and breathe. I know she mourns the lovely prestige that surrounds her mysterious disappearance; the discovery of her car in West Virginia—the hyped up local and regional news coverage, then the near immediate downgrade and dismissal. *The bitch wasn't pretty enough,* I had thought, *for anybody to have given a damn,* and with the world convinced that she had not set foot on this property since September—the property of an absentee billionaire and his anonymous wife—there was simply no need for anyone outside the family to care. The woods around Charleston were not searched, and her car was claimed by her husband, who had admitted that they were not doing well as a couple, even after 20 years. And with that, Mr. Marshall a.k.a. Joe Marshall, stepped into the middle of Suspect Swamp, his feet literally bogged in a rumor of quicksand, sinking, where he languishes to this day.

On our quiet walk among the drifting flakes of snow, these solemn bits of regret ebb the flowing currents around us, knowing what lies in our hearts, but having only the power to go lightly by predestination, to their preordained place under the hidden sun.

These are the last days, as they were in the days of Noah. And there are many signs of his coming—among these being that innocence shall be lost, and the sinful condition of mankind shall be uncovered, to humiliate every sensibility into either repentance, or the ultimate rejection of the Divine. Yes, the world is poised on the edge of Revelation, the tragic unveiling of man's dreadful and perverted self, to lend proper justification for the coming Judgment of God. But whether or not I will be judged right or wrong by Him, I do not—no…I *cannot* care, for I am of my father, the Devil, I suppose—and I have not yet given myself to the Light of a Silvery Moon, and what Redemption draweth nigh. I cannot say whether I love God or no, but my respect for him is Paramount, as is my dedication to my body's lust and sin. There has been, for such a long time, a call from beyond the desert wilderness, to travel to where the Star rests high above, to the place where my future Redeemer lay. From here, I will be transported through time, to where He suffered, bled and died for my soul, that someday I might be forgiven for all the things I've done. But in this part of the epoch, the endless expanse of waiting which is my life, I embrace what I am—whether it be good, or whether it be evil.

And what am I? I am a walking perversion—an abomination of so-called normalcy, as I have suddenly lost my taste for men, and I now savour and devour every bite of another woman's flesh. Is this normal? I don't know. Is it abnormal—I don't know. What I do know is that it is perhaps not *usual*, though for me it is as *normal* as it would be for a man, but perhaps many times more ecstatic to my body. As a woman—my own body parts correspond to hers, breast against breast—private against private—nipple to nipple, clit to tit and clit to clit, and lips to every requisite in between. This Godsend—this woman I walk with now—is a refuge from boredom. My escape from the mundane, my shelter from unfulfilled desire. From the day she first unbuttoned my shirt and slid my nipple into her mouth, I know I have been chosen for a greater purpose, the higher calling of some who bring epic evil into the world, and are protected as they move forward through time. As the cold snow touches my eye, as I flutter an eyelid to resist, I know that how we met, what we did within that selfsame hour was as common as these flakes of snow, spread across the years and miles of humanity. What mankind is capable of, what they do when only God is watching, would fill the pages of a forbidden book, and many more unread volumes beyond. But for us, it is the chance meeting of two closeted *dykes*, with the Heart of the Valkyrie, the Amazon and the Mord Sith, to grow our phantom cocks in the heat of brazen lust and desire. My protection from this cold is internal, I think, even apart from the warmth of my white winter jacket.

As I put my arm around Austria, kissing her cheek, professing my love, my body fades into the Heart of Memory from the morning, when she waited for me at my massage table in tight white Polo-shirt, shorts and big white towel. In the Heart of Memory, I appear in the sunny exercise room, nervous and giggly for some reason as she stands there smiling, looking like a spa employee. It may very well be our first, and totally involuntary role play, as she asks me *"Do you want to leave your bra on?"* I say, "Maybe I should," as she responds *"Well, the straps might get in the way if you leave it on, so…"* and she smiles, looking at me with a gleeful, giddy anticipation which I must return by necessity, embarrassed as I take my shirt off to expose the impossibly big bra, then I reach back and unlatch it to expose the unnaturally big and bulbous breasts (which she tells me are the biggest she's seen since somebody named *Milena Velba*, whom she swears is my twin and the 'World's Greatest Pinup.' Of this, I choose not to know). Though the woman is familiar with the circus sized Sheba's she sees swinging, her big, green eyes get still bigger with unpretend shock, and she shakes her head a little and mouths 'wow' with those big, pink lips. It is a sight that renews itself, I know, because hardly a day has passed that I have not been distracted by what I have seen in the mirror. Whether or not beauty is in the eye of the beholder is immaterial, but whether the boulder holders dig into your shoulders is paramount, which I am used to now that I'm older. Yes, the air is colder on them as they wobble free in the winter house. In sheepish, happy humiliation, I climb onto the massive table face down in the cushioned headrest, staring at the gray carpet below. Then long, warm, strong hands squeeze and rub my back muscles to a tingling—and no, she is not a trained masseuse, whatever that is, but how is the skin of my poor back to know? The best training for any massage is passion. The desire comes through the hands, in every welcomed squeeze and pressing into the muscles. She rubs and mashes and kneads sore pleasure into my back, not ignoring the huge, round masses of flesh poking out from under me on both sides—consequences for laying on my stomach topless on a stiff surface. This rounded surface, both of them, goes unneglected by her. I feel the odd sensation of having them pushed and squeezed upon from behind, until finally she pats my back and gently says, *turn over*. She pats it again, longer and says, *turn over, Babe*. In my hip hugging jeans, belt and no top whatsoever, I do as she obliges. A wide, knowing smile, a twinkling glance at her as she takes one of my breasts in her hands and begins to knead it and squeeze it gently—squeezing it many times, watching the areolas shrink smaller and the nipple push out farther, perhaps just in response to her touch, as I notice when she takes the other breast that the other nipple is still as relaxed as ever. Both of them she squeezes now, pushing them together. Wobbling them separately and simultaneously, then flopping them together side to side like two big water balloons. And then to my grave disappointment, which I delightedly hide, she holds the pretense of massage past where I would have wanted. But what can I do, but relax further when she pours the coconut oil over my raised nipple?

Here, in our walk across this snowy property, my eyes close briefly in a frown, as I remember the desire and despair come together on my nipple just this morning, spreading sensation to my entire breast and to the rest of my body. Both nipples are rock hard now, I see, stiffened by promises—unfulfilled. By wants and needs—unrequited. I wonder if others' breasts are as sensitive as mine—every wobble is like a pounding and driving wind and rainstorm, splashing feeling, crashing a painful pleasuring against the shore. Her fervent hands—the hands of a goddess—splashing back and forth the waters of discontented desire. I overcompensate with my arms up behind my head, looking up at her breasts in the tight shirt now. Feeling the vigorous, rolling waves in undulation, rising and falling back and forth across my chest—compelling me to want to ask her to see if the oil she rubbed on my breasts tastes as much like coconut as it smells. Though she has worked my breasts into a frenzy of flopping and wiggling and wavy motion, my eyes are transfixed on the whited cloth she wears, her white Polo shirt that my oldest daughter left behind, which fits over Austria's D-Majors like a glove. To her quiet surprise, I think, I raise my hands to them, squeezing the firm, perfect breast tissue like I'm testing them…

In the Heart of Memory, I accept that I am a *nursemaid*—a female tit hound, a woman with a breast obsession. I move her arms, moving her hands away from my breasts, then slowly, gradually I raise Austria's shirt, pushing her breasts about halfway up with the shirt stretched tight across them—then they flop hard back down, unclothed. Inside, I am unglued, and my mouth has begun to water. I latch a nervous lick to the nipple of my bitch, then my lips tremble a puckering, suckling pose around her nipple, which I think satisfies her to no end as she closes her eyes, then returns to rubbing my breasts as well.

The flames inside are burning too hot for me to lie still—*let's switch, Baby. You lie down,* I say. Soon, I am at her head as she was at mine, with her lying down, looking up at the floating breast mountains over her head. Her hands find them quickly—she lifts them up strong, causing me to stand up straight, my hands up over my head or behind my back or anywhere while she pushes my tits up and together. Dropping them, lifting them up again. Jiggling them like they were against a jackhammer. It is a new sensation, to have them twiggled so hard, the motion she makes, causing her own to quiver as well.

As I walk with my baby in the falling snow, rounding the grand house toward the back snow covered lawn, the memory trembles my grieving spirit anew, to help me carry the burden somewhat lighter…

And now, I lean forward over the massage table. Pressing my boobs around her head like two great rolling blobs, massaging them, pushing them onto either side of her face while she breathes loudly in between, so that I hear and feel the cool air rushing in her nose. She takes them firmly in her hands, still facing up towards me, and rolls them herself around her face, still breathing in loudly through her nose—taking in the smell of coconut and lotion perfume. But the nipples she still ignores—unblessedly, leaving me standing here above her, squeezing her breasts while she squeezes mine. Taking my new frustration out on her little D cups, shaking and jiggling them with fire.

Yes, the double breast massage goes on in full swing, confidently in the exercise room with the glass window walls on one side, as though nobody in the world could ever see or care. The big curtain, undrawn, rests unused to the side, so that the angels that look in the windows can see clearly. They soon witness me having to sit up on the table, with Austria on her knees up on the table beside me—while I satisfy my soul's craving with my mouth again clamped at her tit, while she squeezes mine like a big sponge cushion. The feel of her in my mouth, and the feel of her hands in deep squeezing is nearly too much for me, and I take one last moan and suck from the Goldman Bosom. I get up on the table on my knees now, on the table behind her as she sits; us both pulling her white shirt off over her head. Behind her, looking at her closely, I lift and squeeze her firm, round breasts so gently, so firmly, rubbing them together up and down, watching her relax until I can watch no further.

Yes. I languish in the Heart of Memory, as we make tracks through a foot of snow across the back lawn. In the Theatre of My Mind, I am at our morning massage table again, laying her down on her back, then straddling her on top, my breasts hanging unbelievably far down, laying easily on top of hers. Here, I know I can find completion, as I look for absolution, rubbing and dragging my tits across hers up and down, back and forth, and side to side, until I am compelled to simply let my breasts cover hers slowly as I lay down on top of her, laying my head to the side of hers. Breathing in pure resistance, trying not to let my eyes roll back while my body jerks one small time, then one small time again.

Yes. I languish in the Heart of Memory, at one with the unintentional trembling from this morning, brought on by our topless massage gone awry. I shudder to think what noisy, frantic grinding and slapping together of bare flesh that might have occurred in the exercise room by the glass wall windows uncovered. More so than she, breast stimulation can bring me to full orgasm, which tends to originate from somewhere beyond my groin, with a slow, sustained power that threatens to pass me out cold when it happens. The sensitivity in my breasts, I have always felt—putting my bras on, taking them off, feeling the weight of them when I bend over, or when I had to lean forward to my daughter's naked asses with paddling wood. And so goes another of mine, having come and gone, this one so mild on the massaging table, but with enough heat to reach forward to now, and melt a few flakes of snow at my feet.

As hot in the pants as a winter walk can be, I step beside my lady in the snow towards our evil door. Towards the back woods of my daughter's fiery dream. The evergreens are all covered in snow from top to bottom as we walk past, gazing into the snowy forest around us. We stand together, somewhere nearby the Divine Will of God, and what Pre-ordination has buried in the snow. We stand together. Un-appalled by the passage of Time. Undisturbed by the flow of events. At the strange depth of easy peace and tranquility.

As the gust of wind blows in from the lawn, we can find no remorse for what we have done, nor compassion for the soul we sent to the other world. As to her body—it will corrupt in time, and return to the dust from whence it came.

"Will you write again?"

"There's nothing left to write," she says. "Nothing left to do but pray for forgiveness."

"You were provoked. She gave you no choice. If you hadn't done it I think somebody else would've."

"What you said about choices... I remember trying *not* to attack her. It felt like I was... watching myself do it. And for some reason, Sarah, I'm just not sorry."

"Did you ever attack your mother?"

"Oh, *God* no."

"Why not? You could've protected yourself. You could have put a stop to the whippings. The beatings. "

"It never occurred to me that things could be any different between us."

"You never thought of calling the police?"

"I was afraid to. Afraid things would just get worse."

"Well, how did it stop? How'd you finally get away?"

"My mother... Laura..."

A pause. A sigh.

"Laura came to my college graduation. I remember being really happy she was there. It kind of felt like the start of something new for us. She hadn't touched me in a while—hadn't hurt me or done anything else. It was in the lobby of the auditorium... we were all milling around after graduation. I had never felt such relief—I was so relaxed—I even think I was *happy*. People were coming up to us like I was valedictorian—I think it was because of her. I know it was. The woman is just... she's unbelievable. Tall. Golden blonde hair, always pinned back. Smooth, white skin. Just enough make-up to drive you crazy looking at her perfect face…

"There was a show I used to watch every week," she says, "called Legend of the Seeker. Dark sword and sorcery type show. Heaven and Hell. Good vs. Evil. Beautiful women. Violence. Very sexy. There was this group of women on that show called the *Mord Sith*. And they were as sadistic as they were beautiful. They were Laura Goldman. Something out of sword and sorcery, she is. Unbelievably beautiful."

"Looking at you, Honey," I say, "I can believe it."

"I was talking to one of my professors—a female professor named Jo Anne Sopperton—she had been sort of a mentor of mine. I think she really wanted me to go to graduate school—she kept saying over and over again, *'It's too bad you don't want to teach—I think you'd really like it.'* About that time I look up, and there's these big, blue eyes coming at me from the bathroom or wherever she'd wandered off too. She motioned for me to come over, which I did—left poor Professor Sopperton standing there waiting for me. I know she wanted to sort of take me under her wing I guess—but I was… 'otherwise occupied.' Obviously. I go over to Laura, all smiles, feeling like this is the start of a new life for us. She just casually, very nonchalantly leans over and whispers something in my ear. She said… *"When we get home, I'm going to beat the Hell out of you."*

Across the landscape of the snowy woods, the words reverberate silently, to shake the foundations of every tree.

"I had to keep smiling though the devastation though," she says. "Through the pain and the fear. I remember at that moment just how alone in the world I really was. And how no one could ever even *want* to believe there was domestic violence between me and that woman. Me and my pretty white mother. Then, Laura started talking to my Professor like she had known her for her whole life. Disarmed the Hell out of the poor woman. She started touching her hair and she actually said *"Wow, that's really amazing. You're beautiful."*

"How did your mother react?"

"She practically melted. The prettiest, demurest show of gratitude you can imagine. Then she eased her way back over to me, all sweetness, *"Austria Honey, we've got to go... remember?"* And just then, I got this vivid, horrifying premonition of being in my forties, still living at home—working at Borders or Barnes &Noble and being beat to death every other night by my mother."

"What happened when you left the auditorium?"

"Well, she took my arm and led me through the noise and the people. Didn't say a word in the parking lot all the way to the car. I was scared, Sarah. But what could I do? She was so beautiful, so strong. I just couldn't break away from her. I hated our life, I hated the things she made me do. But at the same time I loved her. I needed her...

"In the car," Austria says, "I was a little more comfortable, a little less afraid. Maybe it's because I saw that Carolina blue graduation robe reflected in the window before I got in the car. It gave me some confidence. Made me feel like a real person. We got in the car, still really quiet, then I said *"What did I do? I don't deserve to be punished because I didn't do anything."* Then at the split second when I glanced away, I felt something smash me in the face like a book. I saw a flash of light and my ears were ringing, and I could already taste the blood. She had slammed me right in the nose with palm of her hand. She said *"That's what you did, bitch.."* Then in this haze of tears, I suddenly couldn't breathe because she had her hand on my windpipe, squeezing it. I couldn't cough, I couldn't breathe. She said "*Who the fuck do you think you are? A goddamn college professor? If you ever disrespect me like that again I will hang you upside down like a fucking side of beef. You're just a half-white piece of shit,* she said. *I don't give a damn how white you look, you're just a light-skinned nigger bitch with no talent and no future. And I will beat you every day until you've got that through your fucking thick skull.*" Then I felt the warmth in my nose, and I knew it was red. And I could feel it running down my face. Then, when she let me go, I started coughing like I had cancer. I coughed forever while she drove. I coughed until she told me to stop. Then I did."

I don't think Austria realizes at this moment, the tears that decorate her expression, and the look of epic sorrow and humility. Even so, I still sense a strength and power in her spirit, and a sudden mourning for the soul that was taken.

"*Any tears you got*" Laura said, "*You better save 'em. Because you're gonna need 'em when we get home.*"

"Baby, why didn't you just jump out of the car and run?"

"I tried. I really did try. But I couldn't move. It was like I was suddenly in a rolling coffin. There was no way out. So I just shut my mouth and rode home with her. I went in my room and sat. And I waited. I didn't read. I didn't write. I didn't watch TV. I just waited. I tried to pray to God, but I couldn't feel it happen. He wouldn't listen to me. So I just watched the sunlight change color through the blinds, until it disappeared all together. The day faded to the evening, and I remember wishing I could go outside and write a poem, and in my heart, I did. It was called *A Mother and Daughter Before a Whipping*. While I was writing it, a poem I had read years before came to my spirit…

> *"The evening day is deep twilight*
> *Nearby the Edge of Night*
> *Shadows recall fair death of light—*
> *Beyond their feeble sight…"*

"Believe it or not—right after that poem came to me, I heard Laura at the door. She came in carrying all manner of belts and straps, paddles, canes. And a strap on dildo."

A pause. I glance to the Heavens.

Hopelessly.

"My punishment… it went on for hours. She would beat me, then rape me. Back and forth over and over. She beat me and raped me. She was mad, but tireless. She was frustrated because she couldn't… because she couldn't *cum* wearing the dildo. But she kept trying. She kept making me… making me choke on it with my hands behind my back. Then she'd get mad again and slap me really hard and pull my hair, then she'd punch me in the face. I was naked. And she would sit on top of me and punch me in the face until I had to scream. Then she flipped me over and she tried to push it in my backside but it wouldn't go. Then she put lotion on it and she pushed it in my backside, Sarah. Oh, God it burned so bad. It was the worse pain I've ever felt. While it was in, she put her hand over my mouth so the neighbors couldn't hear me screaming. She said *"you gon' mind me bitch... you gon' mind me... "* and that did it for her because I heard her. A woman's orgasm is power. I could feel that power. I could hear it in her voice. Built up from three and a half hours of raping me and stopping and raping me some more. It was inhuman. High pitched and bellowing. Like an animal...

"I don't know if she'd held it back on purpose or not—but when she finally did it—I think it nearly killed the both of us. I think part of us both died."

On the turning of a breeze. On the whirling of a winter's wind, we are suddenly drawn to the edge of our little woods, as if by magic. Across the snow white prosperity field, as if in a far away dream, there stands a figure dressed in black, that resembles my oldest and blondest scream.

*O*ur snowy walk across the back lawn is a long and strange one. Punctuated by the noisy call of an angry blackbird, hidden somewhere from our view. There are times when nature will press itself upon our senses, until we are aware of some anomaly or another, be it the errant crawling of an ant, or the calling of a bird, or the squalling screech and rumble of thunder and lightning. Every noisy squawk of this stupid bird is noise not just to my ears but to my whole spirit, but I cannot bring myself to speak of it. The gray skies above us are darkening, to the growing infinity of snowfall and cold rising, as we approach my daughter in her black jeans and winter coat to match. Black and Gold is the theme; both Death and Prosperity, as told by the contrast between her golden hair and the pitch black winter cloth. In my periphery, I gauge Austria's attempt at a wave and a smile to be heartbreaking.

"You didn't quit school, did you?"

Her non-answer is a somber and meaningful stare, but which I interpret as just more of her spoiled nonsense.

"Dad's inside."

"Peter's inside?"

Penelope glances over at Austria. Knowingly.

"You're acting pretty strange, Penelope. Did something happen?"

This new non-answer is the form of a defeated and bitter, judgmental laugh and smile."Dad wants to talk to you."

"About what?"

"You better come and see."

What the Hell is he interrupting my snowy tranquility for? He is like a black serpent in my white Paradise, in my winter land Garden of Eden. I'm unable to stop myself from looking directly at Austria and saying *"what the Hell does he want?"* I'm glad her look is so perfectly bewildered, to hide the terror in my own heart from my daughter.

Has the investigation made its way back to us? Are the police going to comb the snow with cadaver dogs? How long before the digging machines get to work in the woods? How long?

We are gathered upon the four winds, which sweep down from parts unknown. So weary from their endless journey around the earth. These are winds of what is known—of what is true from the beginning of time. This icy wind blows a warning to me, as we step through the back door of Paradise—stepping as though we are not carried in the wind—as if we can swim the current of time. Of these rivers of phantasmal ebb and flow, there lives a current stronger than we can deny, as it conquers every snowy step, every ice covered precept, every movement towards what truly matters, and what is so dearly meant to be.

We move through this current unawares, following the blonde waif through the mist as the heavy-chested one, and the one with the heavy heart in tow. In this flow we are spun, whirled and thrown—as foretold from the beginning, to nearby the end of this age, to where my billionaire husband stands in waiting, of whom my affection has clouded and rained so uncasually away. Of those days, of those years and love that has faded, there was nothing that could have been done, to have kept our hearts from growing so dark and cold for one another. The fires of this hearth have long since died, so long before this impassioned arrival—and the spirits that carry me to this place along the timeline have blown, to make the air inside our mansion as cold as the winter wind and snow.

"Peter."

"Sarah."

It is as though I don't even know him. A man no taller than my five foot nine Amazon. Thin, with glasses and a Commissioner Gordon moustache, encrusted by the same self-righteous, hypocritical stench that permeates the rest of polite and prosperous society. A man whose sins are justified by hard and intelligent labour, and riches manifested by God.

"Would you mind if we talked?" he says.

"Um... alone?"

"Yes... no... on second thought, I think Austria should be here. Uh... Penelope do you want to stay?"

I don't remember when I have seen Peter Bishop so ... uncertain.

"Peter what's going on? Why are you and Penelope acting so weird?"

The questions loom in correspondence. In league with the attack dog look on my daughter's face.

"Austria, could you wait in the kitchen for me please," I say. With her big, pretty lips tucked in, she rises in the most profound humility, and strolls forthrightly away.

"I don't know why you let her go," Commissioner Gordon, um... 'Peter' says. "This concerns her every bit as much as it does you."

I can only bite my lip and wait for accusations of foul play, and whereabouts of big hipped blonde bitches unknown.

"There's no need to deny it because...because Penelope had the misfortune of seeing it with her own eyes."

I glance at the thing that has masqueraded as my daughter for the past 11 years (since she was twelve years old).

"Penelope claims that back in November, before Thanksgiving... she came into the house and... she came into the house and walked into the kitchen... and she saw you and your maid... together."

The types of fear are many... and uniquely distinguished. Among these is the Fear of Public Shame—the Fear of Discovery, concerning secrets far too private—far too shameful to mention.

The deep breaths I take are cold, and send shivers up my spine.

"And... before you deny anything, I had Penelope submit to a polygraph, and every disgusting question was answered. And according to the test, she's telling the truth."

"The truth about *what*, Peter? I don't even know what the Hell you're—"

"The truth about *you*, Mom. That you're some kind of a closet lesbian. And that you're having an affair with that woman. Don't you try to deny it, I saw you with my own eyes."

Eyes that are red now. Eyes watered by anger, pain. And fear.

"I don't know what it is you *think* you saw, Penelope, but don't you stand there and judge me and lie on me like some stranger off the street. Where do you get off?"

"Hah… not in the kitchen that's for sure."

When someone says the right thing, at just the right time, it has the power of a shove or a slap. How many people languish in prison to this day, by some phantom provocation, slapped in the face by words alone? Sticks and stones may break your bones, but names will break your spirit. My daughter's smart-assed remark creates an energy all its own, as antagonistic as a gunshot. What cold there is has turned to heat, and raises my hand while I lunge towards the girl, and try to pull a clump of her blonde hair from her head…

She refuses to cry out from the burning pain, allowing her head to be bent over while her face twists and grimaces. My other hand seeks out her pretty throat, just as Peter flies on over to her rescue. In an appalling, disturbing quiet, he struggles to free my hand from being tangled in his daughter's hair, unable to do it without pulling harder and hurting her more. Penelope, bent over, finally yells out from the agony, enough to bring out her father's protection—testosterone raised to alarming, as I feel the masculine strength begin to burn my wrist until I have to cry out myself. But as to Penelope's hair, I will not let go. We stand there, in the midst of Chaos, enveloped by the spirit of Violence, which soon takes me over, causing me to begin punching Peter in the face, which begats his full attention towards me, which has him pulling on me with my hand still pulling on my daughter's hair. Soon, his daughter's screams are too much for him, and he anchors her hair with one hand and pulls my clamped hand free with the other, finally tearing my hands free from her blonde-doll do. Whether or not there are strands of her stringy blonde hair in my hand… I do not know.

I move over to the sofa, sitting down amidst the whirlwind—knocked down by a sudden rapid heartbeat and a pounding wooziness in my head. I see Peter comforting Penelope, as if *she* were his wife and not me.

"Even after I saw the test, I didn't believe her," he says. "I couldn't. But after this, I know it happened. And all I want to say is 'how could you.' How could you violate the sanctity of our home?"

"The Sanct…?"

Sometimes, a laugh is born on its very own. It tickles me to shaking, enough so I know they are both staring at my big cleavage in my white collar shirt.

"And how many *sanctities* have you violated, Peter? Fifteen? Twenty? You think I don't know you've been fucking a different slut every year since we got married? *Nobody* goes away on business as much as you do."

"How the Hell do you think I got all this, Sarah, 9 to 5 and home on the weekends? Now *that's* funny. I have *international business* Dear—I can't help if I have to live on the road."

"You do more than *that* on the road, don't you?"

"Don't try to make this about me, it's about you and what you did, and what you forced my daughter to have to see."

"I know what I know, Peter."

"And what is that supposed to mean?"

"It means I've got friends, Peter. And they talk because their husbands talk. And all of you stupid sons of bitches talk about the whores you've been with. How many times have you told me one of your colleagues was banging somebody? You think they don't talk to their wives, too?"

"That's just lying gossip," Penelope says, eyes welling up with tears, "a bunch of bored housewives with nothing better to do than—"

"Shut up!" I scream the words, pointing directly in her face. "Shut your *fucking* mouth before I do it. I'll clamp both my hands on your face until you're unconscious."

"You'll keep your hands to yourself," Peter says. Hands on hips, staring at me like a cop between a married couple on a domestic violence call.

"Who the Hell do you think you're protecting?" I say. "This lying bitch?"

"She's not lying."

"Then, she's *crazy*." I say. "I don't know what the Hell she thought she saw but I am *not* having an affair."

"You are *too!*" Penelope says.

Like an ocelot at an unlucky bird, I jump forward in one last try, but filled with desperation to see her naked and bleeding from my paddling board.

"I said, keep your hands to yourself!" he yells. Shoving me away. "For ten years I've been looking for an excuse and I think this is just the one I'm going to need. It's *over.*"

"You goddamn right it's over.

"And I'll tell you something else too. You're not getting one fucking *penny* of my money."

"Oh, we'll see about that."

"The kids are all grown, you're a proven adulteress—I'll make sure you don't get a dime of my money."

I glance over to Penelope Primrose. Miss Prissy Piss Pot. Enduring the teary eyed triumph in her look.

"You two think you can stand there and look at me, judging me for something I didn't do—"

"I saw you and her in the kitchen!"

"You lying *bitch!"*

'I'm not lying! She was I swear..."

"All right... alright!" he screams. "Enough! To tell you the truth I don't give a damn one way or the other. But you and I both know Penelope. We know it's not in her to make up something like this. Austria!"

"No... no you leave her out of this—"

"Austria, would you come in here please!"

"Okay!" I yell. "Austria go back... please."

Terrified, so much more for her than myself, I concede the defining blow, the deciding cut with the sword, dropping to my knees in the spirit as the Lady Swordsman, to bleed my way out of this world. Terrified, I see the woman in the kitchen—still so meek, so uncertain—turn and move so pitifully back into the kitchen.

"So you're gonna admit it now..."

"Hush Penelope," her father says. "Please be quiet."

"It's true," I say.

The words flow out of me on their own, to grab hold of my poor husband, to turn his head, to wince his face in pain, to bump into him hard enough to make him step away.

"I should've left you on that horse farm where I found you. With this," he says, "there's no going back. I won't even need your signature on the divorce papers. And no…you can *not* stay in my house."

"How would you know if I was here or not? This isn't your home, Peter. It's just a trophy."

Another glance to Penelope Bishop, I take. One last look at the face of epic betrayal. At the face that perpetuates a façade, a ruse of righteousness and moral purity. A face that glows like an angel of light—hiding the darkness therein, the blackness of repressed, passive-aggressive resentment and bitter, caustic revenge unleashed. It is a dish, indeed, best served cold—for it has this special property, that the colder it is, the hotter it burns the skin.

he tone of the ocean is anger. As it stands to reason, while we move towards eschatology. *"The house has already been sold,"* he had said, to complete the devastation, to pick up the rubble and spread it around the landscape of my life. Married or no, the right to sell the house was his—as I have never bothered to care that anything has my name on it, believing that maybe this marriage was permanent, even though we began to despise each other a decade ago. A divorce can be more of a relief than a tragedy, especially when so much of it has been like a bout with a long and painful illness. Part of me had even understood, as I looked over at the broken mess that was Penelope, who had obeyed the spirits that had tormented her for weeks before she gave in, finally calling her father, who was somewhere in Russia at the time. *"Don't you two stand there,"* I had said, *"and act like I'm the only one guilty of destroying this family. Because I know, and I can't prove it but I know what else I know."* This I had said, glancing back and forth between the two of them with insight they both pretended not to see.

"What happened in Fiji, a couple of years ago? When Penelope was a senior at Harvard?"

The question hardly moves either of them, as they are practiced at emotional repression.

"There's something you don't know about Daddy's Little Girl," I say.

"I don't see what this has to do with anything. Come on Dad, let's go."

"No," he says, " No, I want to hear this."

"Dad, let's go."

"Out with it," he says. "Let me hear this lie you have to tell about your own daughter."

"When you got back from Fiji that summer, *your* daughter was different. Even more quiet and reserved than usual. I didn't think much of it—I thought maybe she was a little worried because she was about to go to graduate school. I mean, who wouldn't get a little nervous? Harvard senior. Billionaire's daughter. Wicked stepmother. Wall street future. Lots of life pressure, isn't it? Well, two months later, Penelope shows up one weekend. I remember it like it was yesterday, partially because of how cruel I was when I saw her. I said…*'you're a senior at Harvard. What could you possibly be doing here?'* Turns out she was pregnant."

The shock turns Peter's head directly, to gaze at his daughter as though she had walked the floor naked and squatted to shit on the carpet.

"That's right. Miss Perfect got herself knocked up."

"I thought you were a virgin," her father says.

"I was… I mean, I am."

"I take it you don't need to see the medical bill for the abortion," I say.

"Penelope… is this true?" he says.

All she can do is shake and stare wide eyed, looking back and forth between us as if we were loving, caring parents that could actually help her.

"What are you saying, Sarah? Who was the father?"

I lower my head, half smiling, like an attorney who is just one question away.

"All I really want to know, Peter, is… did you take your daughter's virginity face to face or from behind?"

"You fucking… you ignorant—"

What four letter words, ad nauseam, burn the Bishop brain! What unspeakable insults set your tongue aflame!

"How… *dare* you imply something so vile—so dis*gusting*…"

He opens his arms to his daughter, to which she is drawn in like gravity for the hug. The caress goes smoothly down her back.

"That's right you two. Finish what you started."

"Get away from here you… get away before I put my hands on you…"

I turn in the wake of attack, like an Apache helicopter on the Eve of Victory, and I coast these tragic winds again—drawn away from my husband and my daughter forthrightly, across the grand living room to the echoing kitchen, where the spirits of Melancholy Bay have come to claim another victim: the Golden One, the yellow-pretty, the half-whitened White Hot Hottie and the Woman of Beauty—all encompassed in the single being—hiding in the kitchen corner, as far from the doorway as she can get. Without hesitation, I go immediately to her, to give her the big, bosomy hug, and to absorb what flows from her spirit in epic weeping.

*T*he Earth spins our clouds away in grieving, in the aftermath of icy winds that blow. In the wake of bombs bursting throughout, I step through the rubble in darkness, through the darkened kitchen of my demise, in the white old fashioned, cotton nightgown I love. The woman in white lays a step from one to the other, out the arctic back door, into the cold January night. The sky is as black as pitch, holding the light of no Moon, so that it seems every star in the universe is given place to shine. It is a still, biting cold, frosted by the heavy arctic air around us, and the layer of white snow barely aglow in the dark. The ambient light of cultured civilization glows aplenty, to stifle the far edges of the Truth, which is the blackness of space, and the far flung grace and glory of the Second Heaven.

In socks, slippers and my white winter coat over my gown, I am prepared to endure the cold for a moment, and gaze reverently at the Stars of Heaven. Unknowingly, I stand beneath the Seven Sisters, *"gazing into sparkling light. I watch the earth stars blaze a trail—across a fervent winter's night."* But what purpose—what reason wakes me up with a start and drags me out of bed, moves me down the stairs and to the coat closet in the middle of the night, and out into the icy cold of night winter? Is it the second of the two powerful dreams that tormented me tonight, perhaps even more disturbing than the first?

This first dream had me in the living room of a middle class home I've never seen before, suddenly hearing the sound of crashing glass and bodies slamming against kitchen cabinets; when I run to the kitchen to see what in God's name is trying to break this part of Creation, I see Austria and Susan Marshall in the nude with bloody faces, fighting like animals, teeth blared, locked in a struggling, sensual combat, never minding the broken glass on the floor, slamming each other into the stove and counters, their legs crashing into the lower cabinets with a force I could not have thought possible, with Austria grabbing a paring knife from the counter and jamming it full force into Susan's white abdomen. The sound Susan makes fills Creation with Death, and I wake up on the edge of a scream that would surely have resurrected her in reality. It was too vivid and real to be called a dream—it was a *vision*—sent to me from another world, for reasons I can never fully understand, but some would naively defer to guilt as the source. Whatever guilt I feel for what we have done is beneath consciousness, as I feel fully justified for Austria, as she was clearly and unequivocally provoked.

Yes, words carry the Weight of War, the Power of Combat, and the Sting of Life and Death. But is it a provocation that the courts would accept? Would they understand—who's to say? And what does it matter, when our freedom has been given to us by God, and protected by the angels he sends? I don't know what Susan Marshall did to deserve what happened, but she said the wrong thing to the wrong person at the wrong time; to a Woman of Scars, that had brought neither harm nor ill will to another living soul. Yes. How does one justify a killing? Not the planning of the fantasy of one, but the reality?

Did my second dream point to this reality, in the epic rumbling I heard? The otherworldly clamour of noise, the deep voice of doom in the daylight, which had me going to and fro in a rocking, rollicking house, barely able to stand in the motion, looking for my Austria Lee, but finding no one? As I stand here, entranced by the stars and the dimly lit field of snow, I can still see this same nighttime yard lit up by a Winter's Dream, in the aftermath of what must have been an Armageddon quake, evidenced most assuredly by a fault line in the snow (in my dream), from the cracked patio all the way across the back lawn to the woods in the distance. This dream did not startle me awake as the fighting dream had, but was disturbing enough to get me out of bed and onto this cold winter patio, blowing frozen breaths into the frigid night air—lit only by the dim light of man's lost hope, and the starry nighttime of his faded earthen dream.

I breathe the cold air into my lungs, and breathe it out as a tiny mist of cloud in the dark. And on this last outward breath, I hear what sounds like a she wolf stabbed through, but clearly coming from *inside* the house. Every muscle stiffens underneath this night cloth—turning me, leaping me forward in something that resembles a spirit, though magnificently awkward, by way of whatever is underneath whipping, bouncing and flopping my lose night clothes about, belying all pretenses toward athleticism; bouncing themselves into a rhythm, whopped upward and downward and sideways and byways while I run fast to the steps, admiring my own stupid bravery, preparing me to do battle with whatever hath come to the upper room to kill my baby from me. I fly on the wings of desperation, to get me to the room as fast as I can—feeling none of the steps beneath my feet as I take them one and two at a time, to get to where I hear those dreadful screams come from.

Austria! From whence dost thou make thy fervent scream! Cry! Cry out so loudly in the night, dear Austria, for your Salvation, and your deliverance from suffering! Every step I endeavor, in the hall to the upper room, hurts so much more than the last, each leg now pulled upon by a hurtful and malicious and mischievous daemon that wishes to claw me sore, to make me fall and break my fool neck; that wishes to tear me apart from my new life, from the woman whose life I now am, and whose tragic life is mine.

I run to thee, Dear Austria! Driven by the heat of passion! Lit up by the fires of wanton want and need! Inferned by an unknown passion within! I tear myself away from this last footstep by the watchful eye of the Women of Perpetuity, the Lady of Antiquity in the small picture by my room; from her watchful gaze I emerge to breathe, rounding the corner into the upper room—this room of failed aspirations and lofty dreams that shattered. In this room I take the step into such a howling scream, the scream of one acquainted with the Fear of Death itself.

She is on her back, paralyzed with her eyes wide open, and her pretty mouth besides, her entire body locked into a scream for the ages. The look of fear on her face is pathological, caused by a spirit nonetheless, which I embolden myself against so I can save my spiritual *daughter's* life. *Wake up, Baby,* is the scream from tortured lips, the lips of mine, as I lift up the woman by the arms to sitting, shaking her at first as she looks at me in renewed terror. In her sight, I believe she has been captured by her night demon, and is about to receive the kiss of Death, which will freeze this body to nothing, so that the soul can be dragged screaming into the fiery pit. I can only hold on while she flails and twists, breasts jiggling half exposed in the white tank top, which inspires me to a greater strength of my own—holding her tighter, yelling louder in her face—letting the words *Momma's here!* actually slip out (from whence did they come—this, I do not know!), eventually getting past the chaos, so glad to not have to struggle with a woman as strong as she—her body filled with such rare untapped strength for a woman. I fight this the best I can, getting through the Chaos of Evil, the Spirit of Confusion, of Hatred, Insanity and Fear left over by the demon in her dreams. I press her head hard against my breast, to provide comfort for us both, and the pleasure of a twisted motherhood. *Calm down Baby* finds its way out in whisper—a hushed, low pitched whisper of deception, born from a heart of pure *lust*—though I try to pretend it is only otherwise, as my nipples nearly ache from an inner desire to have them in her mouth. Of this, I know not, I only know that it is Truth, though not unique under the sun, as this plagues many women across the landscape of the matriarch.

"I want you to calm down," I say. *"Look at me, I want you to calm down—"* and upon this chord, there is the somber and fervent caress I take, as I begin to squeeze and massage Austria's breasts so skillfully, so nonchalantly as to surprise even myself at such an act. At this moment, this wretched, pathetic, screaming mess of a woman belongs to me—she is mine to use, to comfort at my whim and desire. To love, yes, but also to possess. To act upon unseemly—and with determined vulgarism and depravity. *You hush, baby*, I say, *Momma's here to take it all away*—this, I say with knowledge of forethought; knowledge that it presses heavy her fearful spirit—carried somewhere deep and far down within—from the place she was born, lived, and so painfully died within.

Upon this possibility I pounce involuntarily, unable to hide the words *I want you to take me in your mouth*—laid so lustily in her ear, to where she is intrigued but bewildered. *Undo my gown*, I say, watching her fumble awkwardly at the buttons, lowering my gown from my milky white shoulders. *Take one*, my voice says on its own, powered by what lies within, by what churns beneath cultured civility. In such fevered humility, in obedience without shame, she exposes one of my gargantuan breasts, glowed so softly as the snow—and she lifts it in reverence, in such respectful, sober obligation, kissing the flattened nipple just enough to ring the alarm bells, driving my insides to a desire impossible, prompting me to open my eyes again and look down, meeting her stare head on, watching her move timidly and with more uncertainty than ever before to my nipple. She puts her mouth to the rising nipple alone, pulling it firmly, to send a tingle to my groin as the desire to urinate.

She continues to suck the nipple alone, until it is the size of a small grape at least. The sensation, I find unbelievable, which keeps me held at plateau. What comfort, what solace does this provide her... I do not know! All I know is what happens to my body when she begins the deep sucking, with the kissing and slurping, and the occasional suction popping noise; all of which soon works my body to a place nearby a precipice, where I am leaned forward in the dark, to begin the falling I cannot deny—which leaves me a grunting, shaking mess of a woman in the dark.

It was horrible are the only words she can say at first—the only truth that will form. It is the solemn engine that carries me on this night train through her dream, where sights and sounds are more vivid than our waking reality. She tells me of this selfsame property, the back lawn covered in snow, but made white under the light of the silvery Mountain Moon, which seemed so big and bright, she says—but still unable to dim the light of a single star— as she tells me that the sky was big and black like over the mountains of West Virginia. Around our property is a forest of blackened silhouette, part of where she is drawn to stare. And though she tries not to look at the woods over the burial ground, closer and closer she walks, stepping lightly through the snow—aghast at the brightness of every star, the proximity of her life to infinity; of constellations and galaxies she can perceive, the precarious stepping forward, along the edges of eternity. What horrors lay, dear Austria—just beyond your vision, in the darkness of the nighttime forest wood? Closer—closer she approaches, until she can smell the needles of the pine, and see the trunks of individual trees in the moonlight.

Run, dear Austria... already, you are told to turn and run, but you cannot, as you are carried along this current of fear, to endure the heavy weight of terror unseen. From the trees over the burial ground she cannot turn away, even when the tattered figure in white stumbles forward aglow...

On the current of fear, she turns, to begin the requisite run back across the holding snow, which seeks to hold every footstep. The *crunch, crunch* of each footstep is louder in her ears now—the ability to look back taken. There is the endless expanse of snowy ground before her, the bright and infinite stars above, the thick and black forest of trees nearby—the great mansion home in the distance—and the crunching of two sets of footsteps in the snow. Oh, how desperately you need to look, dear Austria—turn now... and take a look!

And Fate obliges her grief—with a turning of her head, to see the whitened body of the dead, the corrupted figure of a woman wearing a filthy white gown, a woman of determined malevolence, stepping so determined through the snow behind you!

And now, your labored steps are burdened by the wave—the wave of sound from your spirit, Dear Austria—the sound wave of a long and hopeless scream, to permeate this side of Creation with fear. Run, Dear Austria! Run for eternal life! You know it is what she desires from you—to make such quick work of your body, so she can have your soul! But run all the same, dear Austria—for you are the lying, breathing one—run faster than this Woman of the Dead! The House of Safety approaches— it calls you to Hope and Delusion!

In the Theatre of My Mind—I see Austria nearly leap from the snow to the big patio space, slipping quickly across the tiles to the back door. While in the distance, only halfway to the house, a corrupted figure in the moonlight stumbles forward in the snow.

> *"Earth below us*
> *Drifting, falling*
> *Floating weightless*
> *Calling, calling home—"*

You are calling, dear Austria—for the God you never knew. Take each long, languid step with care, lest thou slip to thine death awaiting, dear Austria. Run over the kitchen floor with ease—bless God for the carpeted living room, the floor of civilization, the feel of home and safety, that divine gift to mankind. Run faster now, Dear Austria, turn the corner to the steps.

Leap them. Take them by force. By groups of two, then a stumbling fall when you think you can leap to a third. No. No Austria—you will not escape, for already you feel the cold rushing in—to grab you by your unwilling feet and bleeding shin—skin scraped to bleeding on the step of thy nearest fall.

Get up, Austria! Fly to the floor of the Hall! Ignore the woman in the big, looming photograph, gazing at you with knowledge uncompromising! Fly past her knowing gaze! No, dear Austria! You are not as Major Tom, drifting home among the stars! You are perhaps more divinely cursed than he, for you are adrift in the current of fear! Fly past the Woman of Antiquity, the Eyes of Perpetuity that stare. Grab the doorway and circle into the upper room! Slam the door behind you with purpose and strength! Slam the door with authority! Now stand there breathing. Listening. Hoping. Praying—

As the arm appears from inside the dresser mirror! And the whitened body of the ice woman crawls out of the mirror, pulling herself in agony into the room! Her arms are scarred from the winter soil! Her eyes are gray and clouded with rage! It is a place beyond screaming, dear Austria, when Death is in the room! When the smell of Death is in the room!

Pull upon the door that will not open! Listen to the voice of the Woman's breathing—

"And that's when I woke up screaming," she says. We sit together against the cherry wood headboard. Me, dumbfounded twofold: One, by the vivid dream she had. Two, by the vivid orgasm *I* had.

"Doesn't take a psychiatrist does it?"

"I think the guilt will pass. You may have been justified in what you did. Even though the law wouldn't see it that way."

"I went to Hell for that book. I was nailed to a cross for it. And if it is supposedly... *'inspired'*, then why didn't I get any help? If the book is really worth reading, then why didn't Fate move on my behalf? If the writing is really good then they would have helped me, right?"

"I read the entire book, Austria. And I think they were all just jealous and sadistic. I think that true talent scares people. It unnerves them. And they're also envious, and pissed off at you for giving them a book better than any one of them could possibly write. Because if they had any talent they'd be authors, not agents and editors. Its ironic that Susan Marshall talked about literary agents being 'evil' and 'complacent', and how they secretly enjoyed denying a talented author an opportunity for success. She said that the very things agents claim they're looking for—a powerful, unique voice, compelling material, sales potential—the very things they look for in a novel are most often the very things they reject.

"Evil and complacent."

"Yes. The very things she tried to deny about herself, are what eventually got her killed. And whether you give yourself up or not, she's not coming back. She might do a cameo in your dreams alright—scare the Hell out of you, maybe. But she's dead. And she died by her own hand. She said after ten years of rejecting authors that should have been rich and famous, she couldn't stand it anymore. So, she ran to book editing. Not realizing that she was running to her death. Tell me... is that irony?"

"I can't turn myself in. I feel like I'd be doing the book a disservice if I did, I don't know why. I'd rather suffer the guilt and breathe free. I've been in a prison my whole life anyway, Sarah. I'd rather die than be put in another one."

"Maybe the book's already served its purpose. If you had never written it, Susan would still be alive."

"I think I'll call it *The Cherry Orchard.*"

"Why?"

"After the line of trees on this property. And something that my character Emily said in the book:"

> *"...I long to walk the Cherry Orchard of my dreams—where the grass is green, and the white blossoms bloom on every tree."*

he Earth flows the River of Time, along the current of grieving. Turning every inhabitant through darkness and light, rolling through the cold and uncaring days of Winter, into the warmth and promise of another Spring. Though we were mocked and judged by every flake of snow, the mercy of Fate harbors no resentment, melting the snow away for another season, to show us a landscape of Hope and Renewal.

We stroll the grounds of our misdeed. Marveling the steady drift of the white Cherry Blossoms, as they seem to flow from an endless reserve somewhere in the trees, which have come back to life for another season. This walk through the sacred grounds is the life's blood of who we are; once, twice, three times a Lady Ga Ga—three times a day it seems that we must step from wherever it is we are, or wherever we have gone, to leisurely stroll the big property, always beginning with the walk down the cherry tree path, where the tale of four seasons is told in the colors of nature's heart.

The purity of her voice is displayed upon every warming and warning breeze that blows, sending the white tree flowers to where we stand and walk, each blossom carrying no ill will, as did the bygone flakes of snow. In each blossom is the promise of another place in time, a place that serves as the doorway to eternity. In each blossom is the smallest grain of Hope, rising past us on the wind, often swirling around us in their sweetest promise that for the accursed, for every living thing, there is a focal point in the midst of suffering: that these things too shall pass—and all things must pass away. And though I am able to rest in the arms of Prosperity, I am aware of the cooling touch of these spring breezes that blow, and the many warnings contained therein.

I have never seen so many blackbirds on this property. Come rain or shine, they take to gathering in treetops in flocks of 10 or 20—noisy crows sent from the bowels of Hell itself, of which Austria cannot be unconvinced, that they are not demon spirits in bird form but merely flying, barking dogs of the air. But so what is it to me, that jackdaws, ravens and crows are drawn like a magnet to bad luck, and that they hang around trying to bring this bad luck to everything that humans do? So what of their desperate, lying attempts to disturb our walks, which have grown in intensity in this early spring, though thankfully not on our walk among the blossoms?

In contrast to the bleak, noisy clamor in the woods and the back lawn, we see above our heads the source of the most beautiful and unique song, which no mockingbird would dare disrespect with their cheap mimicry; the song of the reddest cardinal in Creation, in brilliant contrast to the snow white trees around us. A single red bird, head crested to a point, singing a message at the top of his lungs in a long, arching whistle that swoops down into seven short whistles, then loops again into the single arching whistle that swoops down. This, in beauty without vanity, the redbird sings this message above our heads, that *luck has no morality*, and that *what we deserve has very little to do with what we get*.

There are so many, who are the so-called salt of the earth, who wander through the days in a fog. Unclear. In a haze of understanding with no clarity, meandering pointlessly through life. Never escaping the treadmill, giving maximum effort with minimal results. Trying so hard to do good, be good, but receiving only negative energy in return. Energy that manifests in sickness, poverty and death. These bear the weight of Divine Negativity, the meek and the poor in spirit—the dispossessed and the despised. So much less immoral than so many others. Undeserving of the cruelty they bear, but who ride the Death Train as children accursed, unloved by Fate, whose lives are filled with the barking of the blackbirds, rather than the song of the cardinal.

They are the wives of the brawling, brute force—whose solemn pleasure is to bring tears and sorrow. They are the children of the witch, whose lust burns to the point of violence, to cut with a switch their white skin to blood. Oh, but where is the sign of the cardinal, to strengthen the soul of them who weep? No. These are they who look to the sky in spring blue, who look to Heaven for God's Mercy, but seeing only the outstretched wings of certain death soaring as the buzzard hawk, to bring a charitable end to false hope! Look to the sky, thou accursed, to the flight of the charitable wood hawk, drawn by the flow of prayers unanswered, and the screams of every soul in strife.

Sing, Redbird of Redemption! Sing to those on the other end of the Spectrum of Humanity! Those of us deserving of Death and Dismemberment! Sing our praises of God's blessing, though our hearts are filled with stinginess, lack of compassion, superiority, contempt and judgment for the poor! Though our bodies are filled with sins of the flesh, all manner of fornications and vile immoralities—of this, dear Redbird, of me thou sing! Sing for the million dollar murderers: the war mongers and the greedy heads of state—that seek to line their pockets with the blood money taxed from the pockets of the poor! Sing, Redbird, for the inequities from Eden! For those whose storehouses are bursting with goods, whose vaults overflow with currency, though their sin is on display, on the world stage—set up for every woman and man to see! Sing, dear Redbird, for the Whores of Affluence, spreading new sin to the endtime children, who teach them nothing of God, whose morality is but earthly wisdom alone, to decorate the Tree of Lost Innocence in light! The dead branches are they; this, the false light of earthly progression—the false light of man's wisdom! Sing, Redbird—call out to Austria and me! Call out to the spirits who protect our billion dollar livelihood, In the Midst of Paradise, where we partake of the Tree of Knowledge of Good and Evil! Cry out for us, dear Cardinal, of the luck we must share, as we leave the cherry orchard path behind—to walk the spring grounds in grieving! I hear your weeping cry, dear cardinal, a scream that carries out in song! Cry for those whose heart is broken—although they have done nothing wrong! Beauty without Vanity—thy voice is clear! Tell us what we need to hear—that our lives are blessed in Chanticleer—before the Throne of God!

"The kids convinced me to back out of the deal," Peter says, cutting his steak like a civilized carnivore, devouring it from his fork with carnivorous civility. "They all begged me. They said they loved the house—and they wanted it to stay in the family forever."

"So, what does that mean?"

Across the table, I wait for him to take another bite. Allowing for the thoughtful delay, upon which my own life hangs in the balance. Every patron, every table around us seems lost in their own little worlds, all trained in cultured civility—to display the poker faces in gentility—to cover whatever ills and woes there be sung.

"The kids all like Austria."

"Even Penelope?"

No answer. Just a knowing stare across the table at me. And a sip of Jean-Claude something or another, that truthfully cannot hold a candle to the Welch's Grape Juice in my refrigerator.

"Penelope's exact words were… *'let's not make it worse for her. She must be in a lot of pain.'* Penelope's a sweet girl, Sarah. She reminds me of my mother. She fought for you the hardest, even though you were the most cruel to her."

"You were saying about the house."

"They all agreed that the house was just too good to sell. They *all* called me. Penelope was the last to call. And they all think that despite what you've done—"

"What I've done?"

"Despite your *Lesbian* affair… that you and… *she*… should just stay on the property and take care of it."

"So, you're basically saying, I can keep the house."

"Yes. For all intents and purposes. You are the kid's mother—since their real mother is *dead.*"

The word raises me up in spirit. From the darkened restaurant into the cool night air, carried helplessly, inevitably over the miles to the mansion, then downward to the treetops over the Mansion Wood.

"I guess I should say thank you. I never really wanted to leave the house anyway. It'll be nice—passing the house down to the grandkids."

"Grandkids," he says. "Can you imagine that?"

My mind hovers the woods by the Great Lawn, in fear of what is buried inside. I can see the tall, thick trunks of the individual pines. I can feel the cool needles on my face as I am drawn downward into the nighttime woods. Downward—ever so much closer to the desperate and flattened ground inside.

A bit of steak brings me back, to reaffirm that we are under the Curse of God, in the fact that mankind has a taste for flesh and blood. In this brief awakening, I almost allow the ghost of Susan Marshall access, wishing to be free from the burden of her grave. But if there is one thing I have learned, is that people *cannot* be trusted; a condition they are not fully aware of, that they walk the edges of betrayal like a cliff, and the wrong thing said at the wrong time acts as a stiff wind, blowing them over like a wayward leaf. I know that what emotional trustworthiness we have established here is as fleeting as birdsong, and every bit as fragile as a crystal vase in time.

No. I cannot confide in this man. This Paragon of Virtue here, who eats the flesh of an animal so ravenously, who drinks the fermented blood of the grape without conscience, who builds for himself a storehouse of untold riches, with only the smallest part dispensed to the poor. This man who sleeps with his own daughter, taking her virginity in the motel room in Fiji three summers ago, and still carries on this relationship to this day. Maybe, that is why Penelope understands—why she understands what it means to be so much a part of misery itself. That it might motivate the oddest behaviors, and the strangest occurrences under the sun. What irony must it be, that the daughter I despise the most, is perhaps the one I am the most indebted to ?

The billionaire's phone suddenly rings—something from the Mozart Repertory.

"I'm sorry," he says. "I should have left this thing in the car. *Hello? Yes, it is…*"

At this moment, Peter's expression reminds me of the trembling, towering redwood tree, met with some misguided saw blade.

"We have to go," he says.

Cruising the darkn'd North, in Cadillac luxury. A passenger this time, in Peter's forty thousand dollar set of wheels to nowhere. Both of us busy with our free will decisions—to go to and fro, up and down, here and there and back again. The invisible road stretches out long before us, but silenced by profound disbelief. Unable to accept that we have been ushered onto this motion like cows into a cattle car—free to bounce around inside at our leisure, but destined to go wherever is the train's destination. In silent, severe shock we ride—vaguely, grimly aware that whether we wish it or no, this train *will* stop at Tucumcari; the place where no one wishes to be, but must witness the Angel of Death as he disembarks, to claim another soul in fear, to draw witness from the trainload of souls in terror. We are riders on this train. This journey to Hell on Earth, to provide us a glimpse of outer darkness, where there shall be weeping and gnashing of teeth.

In the dark, we ride the invisible highway, braving the appropriate droplets of rain that have begun to appear on the windshield, lit up by the passing lights that glow. Every drop endeavors to be a portal, to lift and transport me into the Heart of Memory, where I dread having to appear, to be tormented by the ghosts of things once lived. Of this, my teenage years on my widowed mother's small horse farm, where I am rope tied in the nude, breasts bound up, mouth gagged, arms tied together in front to keep my buttocks exposed. These sessions always happen in the barn, away from my two younger sisters, with my two older sisters forced to watch and assist. What have I done—this, I cannot remember. I am in the 10th grade, I know, and perhaps it was a small infraction at school, or a cross look at my mother, I don't know. It seems that my pain is inversely proportionate—that the smaller the infraction, the bigger the infliction. All five of us girls are aware of leather and wood, the nuances of each upon the skin. But these ropes burn a strange and scratchy heat in my legs, around my waists and my breasts, and this leather on my back is cut from the reins of a horse team. Both of my older sisters take part without compassion— my mother holding me by the throat and hair, keeping me stood up straight for the paddling wood that follows, after the white skin of my back is cut to blood. In her face, in her eyes is the presence of pure evil; the quiet, sinister sadism necessary, as sister Sadie pounds the paddling wood into my buttocks as if trying to break the paddle, succeeding only in breaking my skin. I can no longer feel the live wire heat in my nipples where sister Sue Wick had twisted and pulled them while Mother and sister Sadie Wick had held me immobile before the whipping and paddling. *I got ta break ya,* Mother had said, out of breath from the exhilaration alone. Why, oh why won't Sadie and Sue help me! This has been such a slow and steady descention, since we buried our father in the Potter's Field Cemetery. Oh, Father—raise up and strike my mother and my sisters dead, from your grave in the Potter's Field!

In the Heart of Memory, I see my mother's face disappearing in the haze of tears—as I open my eyes again to the present, and see the view in our windshield disappear in a haze of tears and rain.

I am not amazed that our speech is taken in this moment; clamped and held somewhere down deep, where the words merely coalesce into feelings, which manifest into thoughts, which open the door to memories great and small. Of those, I try not to remember the ones that concern my daughters—trying hard to shield myself behind the new love of my life— that golden yellow doll resting back at the Mansion Home. How much of myself have I not confessed to her? Is it fair that she has exposed so much of herself to me, with hardly a single revelation from me in return? Why haven't I told my dear Austria of these memories that haunt me now, especially those of my oldest daughter, who was only twelve when her father brought me home to them? Cute, adorable little blonde Penelope, the quietest and most easy going of the three, and the one I was always the hardest one with the discipline. What feelings of motherhood I had were wrapped up in obligation and sworn duty. A calling answered by necessity—being the wife of a billionaire with five lost children—whose birth mother left with no desire for custody before she committed suicide, not even for the three precious daughters—content to take her 20 million and a promise that she would never ask for another penny, nor would she ever fight for the children she left behind. These five children were abandoned by their dead mother, which left them in the hands of an absentee father, who married me because he got hit with a thunderbolt—that contained in my bra and dark eyed features. Beware the small, picturesque Kentucky horse farm, billionaire! What snare upon it awaits thee!

How much of the discipline, the lack of love I've shown, how much of it came from a loveless childhood overrun with beatings? How much of the burning I have felt in the locked upper room, the aching between my legs when I have disciplined Penelope—how much of this fire was started when I was a teenager—after my father was killed by the horses? How much of this fire of perversion was started by the widow Wick herself—my own mother Wanda Wick, who had burned a trembling lust from her big breasts to her big backside the whole seventeen years she was married? How much of me—the fire that is me—how much of this flame was ignited by Wanda

Wick as she sat on me a year after my father died? I don't think it was something she meant to do—I don't think it was something she ever imagined. How much of this fire—how much of the grinding heat between me and my dearest Austria was started that day on my bed? And I wonder how many daughters around the world have been straddled by their mothers inappropriately, either in the name of fun, or in the name of discipline.

When I have straddled Austria, my breasts hanging down in her face, am I my Mother's own prophecy? Am I the echo of who she revealed herself to be? A closet dyke—an undercover lover of woman-to-woman? Did she herself know it was who she was when she straddled me in her jeans, pressed hard down on me in my underwear as I changed? What is the aching in your eyes, dear Mother, as you look down on me? Is it because I truly have the largest breasts you have ever seen on a woman, though I am only a girl of seventeen? The body is an extension of yours, Mother—unlike your other daughters of various shape—mine is that one in a blue Moon, isn't it? What possesses you, Mother, to lie down on me, pressing your full weight so you can slide your tight jeans down to your thighs? You are not shy, are you Mother, while the sound of flesh slapping together rings our ears in the locked room? I see the pain on your face, as you prepare for what is happening to your body on the horse ranch, in the privacy of the back corner room.

Where does this fire come from, Dear Mother, that presses your lips to mine, with your tongue pushed deep into my mouth, making a sound like what Ike breathed into Tina's soul when he raped her on the movie screen? I feel the high pitched scream, Mother, muffled by our pressed lips—entering my body through my tongue like electricity, going down my throat and into my groin where it will forever be, like an eternal flame of lust unspeakable; igniting my body in blue and black fire. Is this the fire in which I burn, Dear Mother, when I wield the paddling wood to my daughter's skin? Is it what has driven my body in the rhythm of a piston on top of Austria Goldman? Is it what sent waves through my groin and my lungs that day, when I removed every stitch of my clothing to lie on top of Peter Bishop's daughter when she was a Freshman in college, home for the Christmas Holiday, behind the locked doors of the upper room? Did she see in my face that night, what I saw in yours Dear Mother?

Penelope! Austria! Think not of me as a good woman! For I am as corrupt as a Pharisee—bound by a hypocrisy so grand as to be epic, and a morality as false as a desert mirage! Oh, my Dear Austria—how much is unknown to thee! My three dear, sweet daughters—how much is unknown to thee! There is motivation, there is explanation—there is justification, and no condemnation for my sin!

We roll to the lot of our earthly transgression—the nighttime parking lot of the Bethlehem Memorial Hospital. We park in the lights of earthly transgression—the lights of the amaranthine station. These lights are indeed eternal, burning forever in the false hope of mankind—that there is any real help for his dying body outside of God's Mercy—on this side of eternity. These are the lights of our destination—the light of man's confidence in himself—the boastful pride of earthly prosperity and achievement grown, in the guise of medical aid to those in need—a guide to what amounts to a lighted portal; a doorway to the other side of eternity. These are the lights of what Comfort there is for some. And for others, the lights of Fear and Depression.

We walk the lighted sea of cars toward the Cathedral, where the cause of life is worshipped and praised, where the fallen and sick are so laid and preyed upon. As mother and father, we disembark the train—to take the long, dark steps toward what cannot be changed—neither of us able to speak of the phone call in the restaurant that procured us a ride on this Train to Tucumcari, and our daughter's attempted suicide. In times of trauma, life swims a slow motion dream around us, as we become hyper-aware of our own mortality. I watch these doctors, nurses and would be patients appear and disappear in calloused caring and conditional compassion, moving in and out of the double doors as if they had a purpose—as if stopping would compromise the turning of the Earth itself. Among this slow ocean of commotion drifts the billionaire in the glasses and Teddy Roosevelt–Commissioner Gordon moustache, to ask the attending nurse what room Penelope Bishop is in.

I watch the faces take on a deeper and more somber understanding, as if it were possible for them to care, calling Penelope's doctor from wherever he is, to rush to the Connecticut billionaire's side. Attempted suicide by a billionaire's daughter would have to be the talk of the entire hospital, as I see more and more people in scrubs flying through the doors, milling around then leaving again.

Finally, a figure of authority glides through, distinguished because of his age, I suppose. He walks up to Peter, then Peter calls me over to where they are, perhaps to escort us to whatever room she is lying in, so humiliated in her sleep. As supportive as I can, I move quickly across the hospital room, still aware of how slow Creation suddenly seems to be moving. And then, the words flow freely from the jaded doctor's mouth, which have a magic to slow the world to a crawl, where I myself must raise my hands to cover my mouth gaping open, while I watch the Redwood Billionaire begin the tragic lean—where there is the splitting of one thousand year old wood, then the long, slow and majestic fall, followed by a thundering crash to the forest floor. I watch the man's true personality come forth, as he asks the doctor—"*please don't say that... please don't say that*"—followed by the doctor's profound "*it was her time, Mr. Bishop. I'm sorry.*"

Then Peter takes his glasses off and looks to a Heaven he never considered before—calling on a God he never believed in until now. Even I must gauge my own feelings, turning away from my soon to be ex-husband and walking toward the doors, as if trying to get away from a nightmare. I walk out the sliding door into the wet, weeping world, seeing the mist of rain reflected in the streetlights, and hearing the echo in the Theatre of My Mind— "*Mr. and Mrs. Bishop... your daughter is dead.*"

The level of pain among the human population is epic. It is enough to power the spinning of an entire planet, or the revolution of a heavenly sphere. The turning of the Earth, the rotation upon its axis, the rise and fall of each new day—the flow of every rising sun back and forth across the horizon, to mark the passing from one solstice to another. The Earth rolls casually along. A path measured in the groove of space-time—in the fabric that bends it so mightily along. These events are measured as clockwork, to mark the flow of time itself—unaffected by the curse that presses so heavy laden on humanity. The Earth is powered along by pain. Driven forward by the Curse of Eden, the Passion of Gethsemane, to the Fire and Blood of Armageddon. Before there can be Hell, there must be Hell on Earth, which the Earth moves so rapidly forward, in the clutches of the Curse of God. This is the source of the pain we bear, a curse formed by our profound disobedience, and a fall from grace by which mankind is to blame. Every action and reaction—every motive and motivation is governed by this curse; unmeasured by the preordained spinning, and revolution of the Earth itself. The world moves along in service to the Almighty, in grieving to be free of the pain, and the burden of humanity and sin. It rumbles, it breathes, it shakes under the weight of centuries, from the Garden of Antiquity, to the Second Coming of the Lord and Savior. Every part of Creation mourns the weight of the Cross; bloody footsteps on the trail to Golgotha, where sin was borne upon the accursed tree—where righteousness was buried in a tomb, where the stone was rolled away, and this righteousness was resurrected again from the dead. Upon this fading hope mankind once rested, turning so tragically away, as the Age of Grace fades like the sunset, and the light of the Evening Day.

Austria and I languish together in this solemn evening, days after the clouds mourned the passing of Penelope Bishop. The stars no longer haze my vision for her, as whatever tears I had shed are long gone. There is mostly now a profound sense of relief that she is gone, leaving me to wonder if any part of me ever felt love for her at all. What affection I had for her manifested illicitly, behind the closed door of this mansion, and the locked door of the upper room. Yes, I did express myself upon her poor flesh, riddled with lust when she was punished, sometimes until I had to drop the paddle on the floor and stand behind her, massaging her breasts and nipples while whispering false comfort in her ear—not opposed to removing my pants or my skirt when her pain was done. Of this, no one in the world would want to hear except for their own sinful and selfish desire, as it goes far beyond what could easily be understood. It is truly taboo, unspoken and highly misunderstood, that there are indeed some women whose bodies respond to the most benign stimuli—for whatever reason, as did mine when I bathed them when they were young children, and beat them when they were young women. Yes, I am relieved that she is gone— maybe for her as much as for myself. The things I have to confess to Austria cannot in fact be confessed at all, as I am just too afraid of what she might think.

I have wanted to strip nude in front of her and get on my knees in prayer and worship to her, to prequalify my absolution, and tell her that I am no better than Laura Stone— no better than the woman who beat her skin to blood, and raped her when she was twenty two. What will Austria think of me, when I tell her that I have bitten Penelope's nipples until she sobbed and begged me for mercy through tears?

Oh, but what sympathetic origins are these, dear Austria, of the farm where I too had this pain bitten into me! Yes, I am relieved, Penelope, that you are gone! Gone is the epic tension we feel whenever you came home from school, whenever you came into the room. How many dinners have we eaten, dear Penelope—how many have we eaten in the shame of knowledge? How many dinners have we eaten, dear Penelope, in front of your Father and your brothers and sisters, our shame pressed down, repressed down and hidden? The cutting of the steak—the chewing of it, the taste of animal blood in our mouths—the smiles and polite conversation as we swallow the bloody steak—oh, what does your father know! How can you carry this cross, dear Penelope! How much more can you bear? You were twenty two as well, already burdened under the years of upper class discipline, the years of sophisticated beatings—where I had lost my pretense and trembled behind thee, my daughter. Already, you know the sting of depravity, as hands that memorized the front of you, your mother's hands—*my* hands, that played you up and down in every key, until the shaking was inevitable, unwanted, uninvited, unendurable. But you stood there and shook, dear Penelope, to bear the weight of thy calling.

You remember this when you are twenty two, when you laid underneath your father in the Hotel room in Fiji and felt him split you in two! A feeling you did not cherish, pleasures you could not deny. Your father split you in two, Penelope! Unwanted, when you were twenty two! So long he had been without a mistress—so long it built up inside him. Does he know that you have already been sucked and plucked from innocence by me? That you already know the first part of the truth, and a third of you is already dead?

When you come out of the shower in your towel, do you know what your body has done to him? The tall, strong, white body—the milky white shoulders and arms, the creamy white legs glistening, the requisite towel wrapped about your head like a turban? I taught you how to do that, didn't

I, to wear it proudly in false after shower modesty, to hide whatever is or isn't done to your head? Did you disobey me that day, dear Penelope, and remove your head towel immodestly, and begin to dry it in front of him while you talked? You are a woman now, Penelope—hide thyself from him! What does the sound of the hairdryer do to him as he sits at the fine hotel room desk, pretending to work? What is the chiming in his loins, no, what is the chiming in his *groin*, dear Penelope, that makes him take off his glasses and press his fingers to his eyes? When you emerge from the bathroom again, your hair is as long as the Amazon, flowing like a river of gold past your shoulders. *Just like your mother*, he says, un-powerful. Powerless to resist the flow of words from his spirit. *You're still my little girl aren't you*—he says—glasses off, eyes uncovered. What words escape your dumb lips, sweet Penelope, un-innocent, as you toss the brush onto the bed and walk over to him, sitting down on his lap—uncautious. Unafraid. Kissing him so hard on the forehead that you taste the salt from his apprehension. He looks at you. To establish a critical contact, that might begin the chain reaction in your bodies. *I love you,* escapes his mouth, as the pre-echo to what must escape yours. Unjoyful. He leans up, pressing his mustached lips to yours, then grabbing the back of your head and holding you there. Uncompromising. Releasing the kiss. Smiling. Eyes still locked. Then he kisses you again, and this time you let go, relaxing. Unresisting, still in your white towel, hair dried and brushed long and blonde. He hugs you now, teary eyed—un-genuine. Tears designed to lure you in—to make you vulnerable. To make you ask him *what's wrong Daddy?* Then he says, *I just love you so much that it hurts—I need you more than you can imagine. I wish you could be with me all the time. Just hold me—just hold me,* he says. Do you realize what is happening, Dear Girl, as you press your cheeks to his? Can you feel what he is doing, as you volunteer another kiss? Does this new kiss of his feel different, Penelope? Can you accept what it is you have never felt before; this, the burning kiss of a man in heat? This heat coming from your *Father,* as you and he kiss noisily and repeatedly, unable to stop yourselves from having fallen over this cascading waterfall. Can you feel yourself lifted up, Penelope, being walked over to the bed, still in your towel, your legs wrapped so tightly around him? Do you feel the swoon, Penelope, as you are lowered backwards onto the bed, your father pressed so heavily down on you? What can you do, dear girl—his Sweetness is a billionaire! All love and kindness he has been, so devastated by loneliness—what else can you do but oblige? It is but a secret—untold. Unknown by the rest of the world. What is the burning inside you dear girl, as your legs open by instinct, as his hand brushes you down below—what is the air you breathe in, Dear Girl, as your eyes already roll backwards, as he opens his pants and pulls the member forth, as a rod of blue iron ready to burn? What is this you say, Dear Penelope, as *Oh God* breathes from your mouth over and over, as the heat pushes further inside, until it is blocked by natural chastity? What is this agony, dear Penelope, that pushes against the barrier inside, to make you open your mouth as a gate, to let the energy have another way from which to pass? What is the sound you hear, Dear Penelope, as a quick and loud exclaim burst forth as a scream from thee? And now you are in Hell, my dear, as the pumping and humping has started, with the rhythm of wheel rods on a steam engine; the heavy, rhythmic thrusting on top of you, *in* you, your arms now pinned to your sides against the towel, the buckle of his belt cold on your inner thigh. But no, Penelope, you will not be pardoned from the natural pleasure—you will not escape the natural reaction to this action, as you feel the stimulation grow to replace the devastation, the pleasure that grows to replace the pain of lost chastity, and the death of innocence forlorn. Lie there, Penelope, in the bed that you have made; breathe from what is squeezing your insides to contract them— with your legs pressed wide open so you cannot squeeze them together and absorb the blow. The sound you hear now Penelope is your own voice again, in screaming little bursts of sound, to be joined by a wailing, high pitched moan of pure agony from your father's mouth. The masculine strength is unbelievable, is it not?

Yes, my dear, sweet Penelope. My soul is released from thee, under the summer stars of this Connecticut evening. I am glad I don't know where it is that my beloved daughter could have gone. This secret you have carried to your grave, or so you believe, unaware that I am the bearer of every secret. And the carrier, unwilling, of every secret thing.

"*I*'m trying to do the right thing. And you won't let me. Why?"

"I don't want you to go to prison, Austria. You've been through enough in your life."

"Look, I deserve to go to prison. Not because I give a damn about Susan Marshall, but because I killed somebody. And I don't want to spend the rest of my life having nightmares about that bitch crawling out of the ground to get me."

"What am I going to do if you go to prison? How am I going to survive?"

"You still have two daughters in college. Help them."

"So you're saying you're *going* to turn yourself in?"

"I don't know. If the dreams don't stop, maybe."

"Maybe you should write. Just write out the negative energy. Write until the dreams are gone."

"There's no more words. The writing is gone. It was all for *The Cherry Orchard*. And now that it's dead, my writing is dead."

"The fact that she provoked you to that level of rage, and the fact that you got away with it means that it was your calling. The writing led you to me. Then I led you to Susan Marshall. And now she lies stinking in the earth because she spent 20 years pissing on inspired authors and shitting all over their work from pure jealous sadism. Sadistic envy. She was poisoned with it. Any editor who can look at *The Cherry Orchard*... even when it was called *Angels*, and not have the integrity to give it a chance to be published deserves what she gets. And she got hers boy, believe it. She wanted it, she got it."

"Do you think she was really dead?"

"You mean, did we bury her alive? Did you see the trash bag move around her mouth?"

No answer.

"Then the answer is Hell no we didn't bury her alive. Own up to what you did, Honey. You killed the bitch because she deserved it."

"That's easy for you to say, Sarah. You didn't kill her."

"I held her legs. So legally, I did."

"I don't think you touched her while it was happening."

"I didn't?"

"Is that what you're worried about? That I'll say you helped me?"

"But… you wouldn't say that, would you?"

"You know I wouldn't," she says.

Oh, what irony! The sweetest, most loyal and trustworthy soul I have ever met, has the blood of a killing on her hands! As I watch her gaze to the stars that threaten to appear, most assuredly I am aware of her future beyond this life! Yet there are so many, who are pacifists to epic degrees and magnitude, whose eternity shall not be as the woman I see, whose heart is so heavy laden with sin! Whose soul cries out for Redemption—to be freed from the prison within!

*C*an it be said that God made an error in judgment? An error when he created man? But God does not make mistakes—this fact is inherent, in fact. So in what context can the word 'error' be set in, when we talk of the Garden of Eden? For every second, for every brief moment of suffering in human history, I know that mankind is to blame. But what word is it, what phrases can collect to embody the Creation of Man, as it pertains to God's anticipation of our existence? God does not make mistakes, we re-iterate, that fact is inherent, in fact. But because of Divine Integrity—because of his moral completion—our Creation is a decision that he is still paying for, and it grieves him that he made mankind. God's purity is so absolute, that it resulted in a tragic naiveté where man was concerned as he hoped against hope itself, the Hope of God himself—that man's integrity, man's purity would last for an eternity, and that those in the garden would never die. But this Divine Hope was short lived, and the implications grew like a sequoia from a seed—until the wickedness of man was multiplied. What can be said of the Divine Decision—that caused Him to have to suffer, and then destroy his own Creation in a flood? What can be said of the rising of the Floodwaters of Judgment, where the ark was carried around the globe, above the top of the highest mountain peak? I can only say, that whatever mistake was definitely not made, whatever error in judgment that did not occur, it can be said with all due respect for the Almighty, that when he blew the Breath of Life in Adam, he most definitely, *blew it*—to the tune of the greatest irony—that the pinnacle, the most majestic mountain of Creation has been the biggest and most colossal failure and disappointment of all. Even so, mankind is to blame. And yes. It grieves Him that he made mankind.

"Sarah! Sarah!"

I am awakened with a start, from a profound and restful sleep into a world of pure terror, where I can feel an oppressive spirit that I know to be Laura Stone. It is a strong, demonic force whose purpose is only torment— borne from the Heart of Memory, to her dreams. Screamed from her nightmare, out into the room.

Fate decides over Reason. Destiny overrides Indecision. For weeks, I have watched her toss and turn with the tide, unable to keep herself from crashing into the rocky shore of realization, which is the third part of the Truth. From this Cataclysm she arises in the night, unable to sleep, fearful to dream. Walking through the big bedroom in the dark to our favorite balcony, to stand in the cool, North summer night breeze. To accept that the sum total of her life is equal to barriers; walls and gates between her and happiness, and that there is nothing left for her to do but assuage the heavy torment inside. This, the suffering of pure *guilt* that presses down on her like a drill, burrowing itself into the pit of her stomach, until even her magnificent curves are diminished, and she is becoming one of those hot lollipops you see: a beautiful head on a curvy stick.

She can't eat. She can't sleep. She can't write so much as a poem anymore. No more than a person could sitting on a beach watching a tidal wave coming ashore. This is the inevitable wave, that encompasses the horizon of a life, when there can be no escape from consequences, nor decisions that must be made. *What* she had to do is no longer the issue, but rather *how* to do it, *when* to do it and *whether or not* it can be endured.

"Sarah. Sarah, wake up."

"Yes?"

"It's time."

"Time for what?"

"Don't you know?"

"No, Baby. I don't."

How much of it is a lie, that I don't realize why she has awakened me in the middle of the night? In the dark room, there is none of the ghostly fear that has plagued us these many months, but there is the distinct calm of realization, and the tranquility of difficult decisions come and gone.

"What's on your mind, Honey?"

"I don't want to do it, Sarah. But I'm going to have to."

"Have to? I don't understand."

"How long do you think they'll lock me up, if I turn myself in?"

Then suddenly upon me is the uneasy calm in the room—the acceptance of the composer whose mind is on fire with music—the acceptance of the painter whose mind is ablaze with color—the acceptance of the poet whose heart is filled with words—the acceptance of the ghostly figure, who walks in peace among the dead—I understand that this, we must do, if we can ever again have peace of mind.

A blue whale floats along the sky
As a cloud above the evening vale
Perceive the twitch of the swimming fin—
Precede the pitch of the giant tail

"I have to turn myself in."

"Are you sure?"

"Am I sure I want to? No. Am I sure I have to?"

A breathless pause…

"Yes. I'm sure."

"Is it just the nightmares? I'm sure they'll go away."

"How… how many…how long do you think I'll get? Will it be life?"

"I don't know, Honey."

"Will I be executed?"

All I know to do is rise out of bed and go to her, and put my arms around her. The words *ask God to help you* flow out so easily, as if I were truly acquainted with the fullness of Him.

"I'll call Peter. He'll know what to do."

Jonathan Lovejoy

Laura

"*A*White Plains woman missing since November of last year has been found. The body of senior editor and former literary agent Susan Marshall was found buried in an unmarked grave 60 miles North of her wealthy suburb, buried underneath the property of Connecticut billionaire Peter Bishop, in the town of New Bethlehem. Police say that 48 year old Susan Marshall was killed in a fight with female novelist Austria Goldman,*

a fight that occurred after Marshall refused to publish Goldman's controversial and universally rejected manuscript about mother-daughter incest in a small North Carolina town. Although the 32 year old writer, herself a survivor of mother-daughter rape, has pled guilty to involuntary manslaughter, she is currently free on a one million dollar bond, and is not expected to serve any further time in prison. Sharon Norwood...Reuters."

The weight of heavy tension, the weight of years rises. Up and above New Bethlehem, over the Connecticut landscape south. Down through the Valleys of Despair, up and over the Mountains of Disillusionment and Tragedy. This energy flows a heavy southern breeze, cool with premonition. Many hundreds and twenty five miles down east, this breeze carries a warning, in grieving to flow the Coasts of North Carolina where they will gladly be lost at sea—joyful that they may not exist anymore, but will dissipate in time, with so brief a reprieve from misery, before they must reform again. On their journey down, they brush a house in Chapel Hill, beneath the Sea of Carolina Blue.

The woman inside is a soul of bitterness. Borne from her bloodline, and the line of washouts and betrayers in her own life, so rife with failure and dreams shattered like so much crystal at her feet. This woman is engaged by the magazine show, the pseudo-news, the morning frivolity and foolishness. The smiles, the lascivious love of money and fame—the worship of talent, the glory of human inspiration and success. This woman of 49, seventeen years older than the Goldman flower she bore. The Laura Woman. The Woman of Stone. Laura Stone. Laura Goldman.

From the morning news, she hears the words that hold her captive. Words that penetrate her repression, to wake it up in the chiming of her physical body like an alarm, enough to ring her ears ever so slightly, enough to make her mouth water as if waiting for a meal of succulent aroma. Of the tingle in her body—she is long familiar, having once nurtured it on her daughter's flesh, and from the milk of her daughter's life and soul.

On the television screen, the beautiful white Asian talks and drones with such deep and unintentional sexiness; sensuality harnessed and put on worldwide display, to make the news so irresistible, to *curry* favor with the masses, to leave them craving the sights and sounds of her, the lacy tops of black stockings, un-modest—in such calculated immodest display.

Laura Goldman looks at the morning anchor woman. Stopping her by remote. Turning back recorded time, then listening to her sexy drone again. Yes. These were the words that took hold of her mind and body. To make her understand that there is no escape from a calling, and that revenge will forever be a dish best served cold.

$\mathscr{F}$rom the rising of the tension—the weight of years lifted. We awaken in morning renewal. The resurrection of our perverted selves, if a woman loving another woman is truly perverted. Only by perception, I say, as to me it is the most natural thing in the world, which I intend to demonstrate to myself this morning. *I want your face between my legs,* I say. *Put your mouth on my clit—yes, suck my clit like you mean it*—and then I commence the moaning, the clawing of the sheets, as she uses her tongue like a hungry woman on an ice cream cone—until I have to stop her, lest this dynamite explode premature. Or prematurely, I suppose—I can hardly think straight at this moment in time. *Now go back to my clit*, I say... *but slowly, up and down on it until its nice and big, yes... I want you to suck it like a tiny cock, like a tiny little cock...* who else that spent her life in Hetero, is now so Sappho as me! I tell her... *on your knees, baby... arms down...*and I take both her breasts in my hands, staring at them as if they could look back, my eyes aching from the strain of arousal. Then in natural instinct, unnatural, I begin to draw the phantom milk from both nipples, enjoying what I know it does to her, listening to her tell me to please have mercy, as I flick my lips and tongue back and forth over each nipple, then sucking each D cup breast as if it were a soft bottle of warm milk, drawing nourishment as I am programmed to do, as I was once programmed to do. From the end of the sucking, I lay her down to her back, and I slide astraddle—myself grown so much bigger than possible for most women, sliding, grinding every engorged little inch of it against her own until they are locked together in mysticism, exchanging energies we cannot deny, tingling every part of who we are, who we have accepted ourselves to be. I sit astraddle her groin, not moving, only looking at her face and the perfect breasts, observing the golden yellow of her skin, and the perfect beauty of every feature. *Lift 'em up*, I say. *Don't squeeze, don't touch the nipple—just lift my tits up and hold 'em. Hold 'em still, hold 'em still and watch them...* and upon this, I begin to grind so very slowly, finding the perfect position, allowing my hips to find their own rhythm, as I grind her bones to make me bread. *I have to cum soon*, I say, *I'm going to cum real deep. I can feel it... hold my breasts up and look at them. Watch* *my nipples… when I cum, I'll need you to put them in your mouth. Can you do that? Can you do that for me Baby? Yes Momma,* she says. *Can you do that for your Momma?* The giving, and the receiving of such a word, a word with connotations so wide and deep, so high and low, memories that drive and torment us to a controlled frenzy of heat, the heat of a flame we received at birth, the burning of a flame as blue as the ocean, and as black as the night we hearken from. This burning, this fury of blue and black fire, this raging inferno from our mother-lines, moves my hips in a sliding, a rhythmic gliding I can no longer control. *Hold 'em… hold 'em and look at 'em… your Momma's cumming…* and from somewhere along the timeline, the rumbling goes through me like Jello in an earthquake, shaking me to the core of my human spirit, pushing a loud and gruff bellowing from my lungs while I struggle to hold on, unable to see or think rationally in the storm of energy, rolling like a hurricane from inside my womb, up through my breasts being held still, and out through the strong, wet pulling suction I feel at the front of them.

"I think I came in my tits," I say laughing a little, shaking my head. "I almost passed out."

"You lost your mind," she says. "Your eyes rolled back a little, and you started babbling."

"Babbling?"

"Something about your Momma. Or my Momma or something."

"Oh yeah… you called me *Momma*. When you said that, my body went crazy. There were like, two points of energy built up—when you sucked my nipple, I swear it felt like I was coming in my whole body. I could feel it striking every time you sucked—it felt like you were nursing 'em."

"Like a baby, I was. I went for broke. And apparently, it paid off."

"I swear I've never felt anything like that before in my life. I'll bet you it'll never happen like that again."

"We're certainly gonna try though, aren't we?"

"No… no please Honey no more."

"I didn't get mine, you know. I'm still horny."

"You'll get yours later."

She smiles, rolling back over onto her back, suddenly lost in thought.

"You alright, Baby?" I say. "If you really want to we can—"

"No, that's not it."

"I can't believe it. What you've been through… but it's over."

"How?" she says. "It's some kind of a miracle or something. I thought I was going to jail for the rest of my life."

"Those lawyers aren't millionaires for nothin'. I told you, you had to have Faith. The second you told me you had to turn yourself in, I knew it would work itself out."

"Not me. How close was I to life imprisonment? One wrong look? One wrong word? What if they knew I hit her first? Or that she never really tried to choke me? Or that you held her legs? How close was I to the other side of Paradise, which is Perdition?"

"Accept your Fate, Austria. It was a calling. As surely as it was for you to write that cursed book, you were literally *called* to kill that woman. It's not something you could have ever imagined yourself doing. But you did it without hesitation and without remorse. And without a second day in jail either, by the Will of God himself. Something took hold of your mind and body… to execute this woman. Tell me, are you sorry you killed her?"

"I… I don't know. Part of me is, but part of me realizes that I had no choice. The things she said to me. Even now I still can't believe she would stab a fellow literarian in the back like that—and then just walk away because she suddenly didn't like the book."

"Well, it's obvious that she was full of shit. It's obvious to the whole world now. This was meant to be, Austria. Because you walked onto this property at the twilight of your perseverance—at the very end of your rope."

"My faith in the book was gone, Sarah. It still is. I'll have to see this before I can believe it."

"See this…" In the next moment, I circle my finger in the air, then down and around, until the ghostly form of a nine sits in the air.

"I know," she says. "Nine publishers."

"There is a bidding war for this novel, Baby. And you'll never guess who wants it the most."

"Susan Marshall."

"Susan Marshall's *ghost*." I'm suddenly racked with a cruel and hearty laugh. "She… she floated back to her agency and said *Emily…*" 'Emily' rolls out in that high pitched, comic ghost voice everybody can do.

"Emily?"

"That's the character in your book isn't it. Emily something."

"*Emily…*"

I watch the wheels of her mind begin to turn, to tighten her expression, brow wrinkled, eyes piercing something only she can see.

"What?" I say.

"Nothing…"

"Come on, what is it?"

"Nothing. For a second there, I thought the book had a new title. Irony is a real bitch, isn't she? Here I am, in the lap of luxury without a care in the world, could care less if Emily ever gets published, and now there's a fucking bidding war for it—"

She pauses, then holds her bare stomach through the painful laughing. "I fucked my mother."

Another burst of insane laughter. This time, from the both of us.

"Me too," I say. To tickle our hysterical bones again.

"Wait a minute," she says, sitting bolt upright, naked as a newborn. You were just kidding right?"

"Remember when I told you I never even saw my mother naked?"

"Of course."

A pause. A deep breath.

"I lied."

"After my dad died... my mother lost it. She whipped us five girls all the time and for every little thing. Whippings were simply a part of who we were. We even had to help her sometimes, and if we didn't do it hard enough she'd whip us for that later. I can remember hugging my older sister and crying after one of those, begging her to forgive me. She said she understood and that she forgave me but, I could see the pain in her face.

But what could I do about it? What could any of us do? Well, one day my mother stripped naked, and made me do the same. After she burned me up with the leather belt, she hugged me. There we were in the bedroom, behind a locked door—naked as two skinny-dippers. I remember my skin was on fire—itching, bloody scratches and scars all over. Our breasts were mashed together."

"How did it make you feel?"

"Weird. That's the only word for it. But my mother was very pretty, shaped just like I am—big, giant breasts, small waist but with really big, wide hips, very much like that true hourglass. My butt wasn't quite there yet but my tits were huge by then. I was only sixteen and my F cup bra was too small. I think my Mom was... I think it was as simple as... I think she was just eaten alive by pure lust, Austria. The kind of thing you read about in erotic fiction and you just don't think it exists but it does. The way that there really are mob hit men sitting in prison, there really are some real world mothers sitting in a prison of perverted lust. Of course, you know that better than anybody don't you?"

No answer.

"I don't think it was anything wider or deeper than that. It was just a lust so strong that it pushed her to punish us girls like there was no tomorrow. And one day it just picked her up and carried her over a line she probably had never really knew existed before."

"What did she do?"

"She got in front of the mirror and made me get behind her. And when she bent over, I could see her... her vagina. It was huge... I still remember. She had obviously gotten so aroused from the whipping that she couldn't take it anymore. She told me to press myself against the back of her. She told me to bump up against her until it *feels too good*."

"Did you?"

"Something took hold of me. I don't think it was two minutes before I was shaking. Then she put her hands between her legs, and when she came, I remember thinking of the horses, and how much power is in them when they jerk and twitch. She lurched backwards against me so hard I almost lost my balance. I held onto her the best I could. Until she finished. There she was… leaning on the dresser, totally spent. Face flushed, mouth open, eyes half closed. She looked like she was about to faint and you know something… neither one of us had made a sound. Except for some serious heavy breathing. And I can remember that Mom had put her head down and had knocked stuff all over the dresser trying not to scream. I honestly thought something bad had happened. But then she stood up and put my hands up to her chest. We went over to the bed. She laid me down and straddled me, barely recovered from the first one. She put her hand around my throat so she could get off again. Then she told me to hold her breast up and '*suck her titty*', as she put it. She ground herself to a second orgasm. With her hand around my throat. Her body was so strong, Austria. Sometimes I think she was as strong as a man. Do you know what I mean?"

When I glance at her, her thumbnail biting and lonely, plaintive stare are the only answer I need.

Jonathan Lovejoy

"*W*hat are the jangling keys of discontent? What are the clanging discords of despair? What is the cold that descends upon my nerves like a breath of night under a Winter Moon? From the sunrise of this early morning, throughout this ordinary day, to the passing of

222

Sol through the Western Gate, even to the shadows that have reached out to us and died, I have felt the approach of this impending night with a dread deeper than any I have known for quite some time, as if I am aware of an approaching menace just beyond the horizon, but can do nothing to stop it, escape from it, or ascertain the hour of its fearsome arrival. It is the approach of an invisible wave, a wave of total devastation—like the blast wave of a nuclear explosion that leaves nothing intact for miles around, though its approach is as clear and transparent as air. I can hear it, I can feel it, and I know of its impending arrival, and of what lives shall be gathered up and gone.

What are the jangling keys of discontent— what is the unbeautiful score of dissonance, to mark the tragic arrival along the timeline? Why is it new that the feel of her straddle against my groin, the smell of her, the burning heat of her fire drives me further away from what I know as a form of sanity, like the swimmer lost in the middle of an ocean trek to a shore she can see afar off when the sailboat is capsized, but now the stroke of effort has left her insane with agony—the pain shooting through her arms and lungs, the anguish of her husband and children foolishly left behind while she sneaked out for a sail—all of it working together to produce a weight on her now, a burden too heavy to carry another mile through the water—a battle too insurmountable to climb to victory—a rip current too brutal to challenge any further. Swim, dear woman, glide parallel to shore like they told you! Never mind that you are being pulled further out to sea! And thy stupidity is as grand as the sun that has turned orange behind you! To add to the weight that is such a tragic burden to thee! I am this poor woman, yes, a woman of a full 35th year, sitting back on my bed in the evening day, unmoved by the strength and power of the 55 year old woman of beauty, who sits astraddle me, facing my feet—sitting so still as she is able, despite the growing ache in her body which has started in the long, swinging breasts whose nipples I tweak, whose nipples I pull and massage without ceasing, knowing that after a half hour of this, the ache will connect to that in her womb, to spark a river of lightning that will hold her in Divine electrocution for many long and pleasurable ticks on the time clock. I can sense her growing frustration—yes, I can hear it in her voice which she has now let overflow into the small space of our southern room—pressing herself down harder on me, until it is easy to imagine what I know has grown four inches from inside her—a clitoris that enlarges itself to the Sapphic Cock of Legend when she is aroused, as though she were born to attach herself to other women. To me, she has attached herself underneath cultured civility—to release the pain built up inside of her—an agony of carnality too severe for any man to have even begun to understand, nor would she have wanted them to. These years of public chastity have been a ruse—a false face put on for her Christian friends, one of whom has interrupted a secret punishment unawares—which brought the word *goddammit* from her mouth so quietly, when she had to put the paddle down and answer the door—telling me not to leave the room no matter how long her Christian friend should stay. Here, in my 35th year, I squeeze and squish, twist and tweeze, bobble and please the Devil out of her big, long tits, still amused at the heavy weight of them, driving her like an exotic vehicle toward orgasm with only my hands on her breasts, pulling at the nipples again just so, noticing her lower her head and let out a long breath, as if it has pushed her forward just enough, to cross the terminator into night, beyond where return to day is possible. This, the darkness of full on Mother Daughter Perversion, which pervades the world like the air we breathe but is every bit as invisible, and unknown to the naked eye. It is the last taboo of improper speech, the last place polite society refuses to go—unwilling, or unable to accept the commonality of this unspoken act, though it has risen up in modern times to affect even the public Mother-Daughter Dynamic, where women of 55 no longer surrender their sexuality. But for some, this spirit, this Mother-Daughter Lust, is suppressed when they are together in public, and for an alarming number, is fully expressed so willingly in private. I am among the unfortunate, among those who have seen—who have been through this barrier, to where motherhood is no longer sacred, and there are no more leaves upon the Trees of Innocence.

I tweak, I pull, I squeeze and I pinch the Nipples of Venus again—this time to the tune of labored breathing from my mother's mouth, then a deep and pitiful wailing, a mournful moaning that sounds as though she is weeping from deep inside, every sob brought on by the nipple tweaking alone, which has sparked as lightning to her womb and her groin. These are the sounds of despair; activated by the energy swirling from both her breasts to her groin and back again—a tension now attacking her body in waves as she sits on top of me facing my feet, my fingers still teasing both her nipples without mercy.

Mother, thy punishment has begun! No, I will not release your body from this latest trauma! You will suffer the crying pain of a breast orgasm, such a rare and special place along the wide and crooked path! Such arousal can only be known to a blessed—or rather an accursed few! The idea of your daughter being the fuel, the source of this black fire tinted blue, the idea of it compels thee! You are a woman bound busty to a chair of deep perversion, your arms behind your back, breast tightly banded and bulging, mouth gagged and eyes closed in sweet surrender! It is a fire burning so hot Mother, a blue Fire Devil, a tornado of blue flames along your desert wilderness of night! Now, jerk inside those flames, Mother Dear, let the crying inside your voice transform itself to the gruff, rough grunting in the aftermath. From the nipple tweaking alone, Mother—thy evolution is complete! Now rest a while, Dear Mother—lift yourself up from the straddling. Turn to me on all fours now, your big, white breasts hanging bulbous and long. Are you aware of the wet linen, Mother Dear, where thy devastation hath drawn the water from thee! Crawl up to your daughter, Dear Mother…crawl up to me. Lie down with me. Rest a moment, though the lust you burn is only two thirds gone. Let it rest a moment—let it build up enough. Lie still, dear Christian woman, until you cannot lay your beautiful head any longer. Lying beside me, you move your head to my breasts, and I cannot resist the spark in my groin, when you pull my nipple into your mouth. Mother—I am tired of the feel of your tongue at my nipple, the sucking that draws the innocence from me like a sucking tiger cub at its deadly mother's milk. Of thy milk, I am tired of the taste of it; the taste of your sweat, the taste of your arousal, and the smell of your cunt in my nostrils. Go on, suck my titty, Mother. Suck it dry of what hope there is left for you and I. The feel of my breasts in your mouth takes you back to that place, doesn't it?

Mother slides her leg over mine, and soon she is on top of me, and we are engaged in the full kiss—which I am practiced to be aware in, to feel her tongue probe my mouth to my throat, as we engage in the deep, sucking kiss, Mother to Daughter, Woman to Woman, Heart to unresisting Heart. The grinding has begun, where her soft cock will emerge from hiding again, secret and sensitive, each grind causing it further sensitivity—her whole body already beginning to rock in vigor on top of me, grinding me down in missionary, where I am unable to stop the swelling from within myself, to meet her where she lives, and connect our misery one to another. The woman on top of me gathers her strength by necessity, to attack this steeper cliff to climb, where the peak is harder to reach, with more suffering effort to achieve. Her back is hunched, her head is tucked close beside mine, her arms are anchored to each side of me to give balance, as already the masculine strength has begun to flow through her woman's body. The possession has taken over this mature woman again, who has begun to pump and grind her groin to me as if to stop would mean certain death. Her voice whimpers in my ear for me to grab her bottom, and I oblige—sliding my hands from her small waist to her wide, bubbly bottom. *Yes, grab my bottom*, she says, still unable to speak the word *ass*, even from the pits of private perversion. With my hands on her big, wiggly ass, we are a machine in unison, my arms as the wheel rods of the engine, measuring the rhythmic pumping of her hips slamming and grinding, her voice whimpering louder a quiet insanity she cannot control, until I hear the *'oh, no'* escape from her mouth, and then a single, helpless yelp, followed by the stiffening of her entire body, then the shaking, then the jerking and convulsing and the rough, gruff grunting again. This second climb has left her spent, along with myself, trapped underneath her, buried alive as beneath the rubble of a building after an earthquake.

As I lay dying underneath her, my own body racked with an unresolved arousal, unwanted, I feel the arrival of the blast wave from my evening horizon, and I know now that there can never be another foray into this darkened woods, and I know that soon, by my hand, either me or this Christian woman on top of me will soon be dead."

*W*e emerge from the dream of another orgasmic stupor, the two of us, one that has lasted through the night, where we traded missionary superiors into the early morning light. We are both driven forward now, seemingly all the time—throughout the day and into every night—by a lust so powerful that we can mount each other's legs like dogs if we want at any time—a lust stronger than even we had thought possible—that has married us to one another in both mind and body. We prefer clitoral stimulation to vaginal penetration, as our spirits are so inclined, as our maximum sensation is the fevered missionary grind. Bras on or off— underwear up or down and away, the merging of ourselves from the waist down has become our desperation, until we have had to concede that we're rubbing ourselves raw. But these spirits that torment us must be obeyed, as long as we are together.

Even at the cooking stove this morning, fresh and safe after a shower, with so-called new clothes on for the day, I had to move the eggs from the heat and be there for her when she walked up behind me and breathed in my ear—*I can't help it Sarah. I'm sorry*, and I was inclined not to judge her or resist her as she undid her belt and slid her jeans down, then pulled my shorts and underwear down and white pullover up. I stood there earlier this morning, watching the eggs burn, feeling Austria slide one breast out of my bra then grabbing on to it. I had stood there fascinated, enraptured by the moment more in my mind than my body, as I felt this woman holding onto my breast for dear life, stopping once only to insist that I put it in my mouth, which I did briefly, along with the obligatory moan, which sent her quickly over the line, and her groin slamming into the back of me became involuntary almost at once, until I felt the masculine strength in her woman's muscles, and heard it grunting pitifully in her voice. I had stood there, denim shorts half down, shirt up, one breast out, fascinated by the power of lust, how it can grip a person's body, and drive them forward to do the unimaginable by instinct. Not many times at all, she had slammed into the back of me until her need was met, and I had stood there, glad to be the outlet for what she needed. I had stood there. Enjoying the passion, the irresistible craving she had displayed, her trembling fingers at my bra like those of an addict in a locked bedroom fumbling with the pipe or the pills. I had stood there. Staring down at my nipple, un-erect, feeling her chest rise and fall against my back, listening to her warm breath in my ear.

*L*aura Stone drives the miles. Laura Goldman. Parking the champagne Taurus in the airport lot, after the Road of Contemplation. Stepping out of the car—Capri jeans, black t-shirt so appropriately in place tucked in. Golden hair pinned back slick—eyes pale green.

Under the summer Carolina sky—Laura Stone walks through the airport parking lot, rolling the bag behind her. Pulling it along. Laura Goldman. The looks and stares bear it out. But no. She is not a stewardess. Nor an actress. Nor a model. She is a mother. Alone.

Laura Stone travels the miles. Laura Goldman, in the air of Carolina blue. Gazing out the window over the right wing. Knowing what it is she has to do. Having already searched her heart from the roads of Chapel Hill, to the skies over Raleigh-Durham. Knowing now that her one way ticket North has been justified already.

Laura Stone flies the miles. Laura Goldman. Enduring the chatter from the plain mother beside her, who rattles on about her beauty, the words "I thought you were one of the stewardesses" requisite. And now, she feels the looming clouds over Connecticut—the towering mountains of fluffy white. She gazes with eyes of green, descending, seeing the clouds climb further up and away, as she rides a little lower than the angels. Rolling wings of freedom across the ground. Down the runway of conviction. Toward the path of freedom. The path to victory.

Laura Stone disembarks her windy chariot. Laura Goldman. Taller, stronger, prettier than every woman in sight. Finding her bag in the airport. Rolling it along again. The black bag of purpose. The luggage of determination. Not considering the name of what goods she has gathered inside. What type of so-called kit it would be.

Laura Stone walks an airport lot. Stepping the tired asphalt again—to a car she has never seen. A rental. A Taurus so unlike the champagne car she left behind. Newer. Uninspired.

Black bag in the back seat now. In the rear view mirror, she gazes eyes of green. Forty nine years of aged and seasoned beauty. Unadmired. Unrepressed.

Unbridled.

The chiming of the bells brings the melody in sweetness, that of the sonata facile. I glide through the glass doors from our refuge on the back patio, convinced that this is another interruption from the line of onlookers, the reporters and literary agents and editors all desperate for a piece of Austria's cherry pie, and what lucrative promise and pot of gold may be found in *The Cherry Orchard*. I am already prepared to tell whoever it is that the spot on this train has already been taken, and the book has been sold to a publisher for an undisclosed eight figure amount, the largest advance in the history of publishing, and that the author is unable to give any interviews, about the novel that went from 'Angels' to *The Cherry Orchard* to 'Emily' and soon to immortality. The novel that caused a woman to die already, about a thirty five year old woman who had been beaten and sexually abused for twenty years by her suburban mother in a small North Carolina town. Whether this advance can be justified, only time and future history can tell, as Austria herself has thanked the Almighty that she no longer cares, and that 'Emily' now belongs to the rest of the world.

And when I open the door, the smiling face and beautiful eyes remind me that some clichéd expressions are true regardless, as classic as what they represent, which is why they were worn out in the first place, as *the blood in my body does indeed run cold*, from my heart, down to the bottom of my feet.

"Mrs. Sarah Bishop?"

Standing before me, as the substance of a waking dream, is the demon of every dark fantasy. The angel of Hellish imagination turned outward, having spewed itself into reality.

"I... excuse me but... do you know Austr... I mean... Lee Goldman?"

She relaxes the prettiest bottom lip, red in lipstick unafraid to be feminine, to reveal a flash of a set of bottom teeth white enough to create anguish to see them again.

"I'm Lee's mother."

I have met too many people in life. Been everywhere—seen everything. So I know that I'm not conditioned for shyness at meeting new people. But for the first time as I can remember, the meeting of a new person has left me fumbling for lost confidence, and stumbling through a cold darkness in fear. But from somewhere deep down, from what can only be called courage, I suppose—the perseverance of a terrified soldier in battle—I find the strength to step forward in false civility, smiles and *fungalooga* greeting—even the requisite and ridiculous hug that makes my cold bowels ache.

Beauty is the most underrated quality known to man, yet it is the source of man's total desperation toward one another, of which women cry themselves to sleep in prayer to possess, as do men to possess the women who have it. What I see walking beside me, is truly the most beautiful person that I have ever seen in real life—the craving of Madison Avenue, the lust of every Hollywood fantasy in real life, and the pain of every starving and well fed artist ever known. Hers is a beauty that cannot be ignored, as is the actress that rules the television, or the motion picture or the print ads for a generation, to cause people to not believe that they even exist in *real life,* because through all our middle and upper class mediocrity—it is *beauty* that is rarely or never seen in person. What I once thought was beautiful when I looked in the mirror has been irrevocably altered for the rest of my life, and I find that I cannot stop smiling and staring, and acting as though she is my best friend, come back from a journey she started long ago.

Phoniness and hypocrisy have their roots in fear. Fear of being judged or ridiculed ourselves, for presenting the truth about how we feel, or fear of causing offence or insult, or simply being afraid of the truth itself, which can swing a cold blade through the soul, to leave one in devastation and ruin. And I walk past the white room in fear, with all superficial questions stacked neatly in place, to do battle with the demon of uncomfortable silence, to lay waste the monster of social awkwardness, to walk in pure betrayal towards the patio door in our grand kitchen, unable to move my body to do what its right, but only what is proper and polite. In sheepish, giant breasted politeness predestined, I slide the big glass door open, having to call the soon to be famous author's name in the only warning I'm bold enough to give. The beautiful young woman turns her head, and I am a witness to the miracle of non verbal communication, as I watch her eyes widen, and her mouth drop open like Laura Dern's did in Jurassic Park.

*W*hat have I done?

Sometimes, this sentence rings like a chorus through the mind, as it did when I stood over my step daughter's grave, and when I allowed her guilty father to blubber in my arms without confession, both of us admitting through catharsis that we "should have been there for her." Or did we only give a damn about ourselves that day? What loss I felt for Penelope was buried with her, and what I felt when she died was only the nagging guilt of having abused a young soul to the grave—the same guilt one might feel for an animal run over in the street that you had never seen before or would ever see again. Yes, this chorus played in my mind that misty morning, when I watched Peter Bishop lay his beloved daughter to rest. Would her natural mother have attended her burial if she were not dead herself? No. And why should Mary Bishop have visited the scene of a crime she committed years before? It manifested in her daughter's life, having left all five of her children, agreeing to a 1 million dollar a year stipend for twenty years if she never saw them again, because a hidden camera in her bedroom caught her serial adultery on tape. Over 80,000 dollars a month cash, and a signed confession of adultery, signed divorce papers, signed away custody, and signed checks saved enough to make her a millionaire five times over even before she became a sixth grade teacher with a new husband and two new children of her own. Before she took the pistol from her husband's gun collection. Small price to pay, for a *cheating bitch of a wife*, which Peter had said in the arbitration room as he signed the financial agreement, which brought only a smile of victory from the blonde bombshell, who had cranked *"those five brats"* out just because her billionaire husband had wanted them anyway. Five accursed children, who had come into the world unwanted, who had been looked after by their birth mother as a disinterested nurse. Five accursed children, who had felt the pain of parental neglect all their lives, including one who was buried at New Bethlehem Cemetery. *What Have I Done,* was the refrain at Penelope's grave, as every scar I left was lowered into the ground with her.

And as I watch the most beautiful woman in Connecticut glide an Amazonian body across my patio, as I watch the light skinned woman of like beauty stand in fear, her expression gone to hound dog droop and a somber frown, as though she has become sick to the pit of her stomach with fear—as I watch her face twist in the battle to hold back the tears that begin to run—as I watch the beautiful mother reclaim the daughter she held in a captivity only imagined but never believed, the refrain plays in my head like a Chorus of the Leaves, where the harmonies breathe torment to every corner of my spirit, soul and body—*Oh, God... what have I done?*

I pull myself from the quick sand I mired myself in, to take a fool's step toward the two of them, until I'm beside them close and intimate. There are no tears left for me to cry, but my grief and fascination are infinite nonetheless; seeming to call forth a strong and cool summer breeze, one that gives voice to the cherry trees that stretch the length of this back property, even the evergreen woods across the Great Lawn, and the pines above the empty grave. Creation itself, at least this small part of it, has *got* to be aware of this meeting, this meeting of the minds, the quiet crying of the Mother-Daughter Dynamic, the mind of a sexual sadist, and the daughter she bore and raised.

And as Austria begins to sob, I am un-inclined to recline away, only to breathe in deeply, and place my bosom upon their natural incline. And I step boldly around them so that I can see the face, the eyes of this beautiful sadist, and whereabouts she gets the balls to come here, and hold her crying daughter in her arms. This woman, who thought it nothing to strip her adult, college freshman daughter naked and beat her bloody with her dead father's hard leather belt because of a cross look when she asked for her help doing the supper dishes. People think that such punishments for such minor and manufactured infractions are the stuff of trash and fantasy, but I am a living witness to the contrary, standing in front of me in a black t-shirt and capris pants, hugging her daughter who sobs. I cannot suppress that hypocritical judgmentalism, that false charity, that phony protectiveness born from pure jealously alone, that my woman is pouring her soul out like this to another.

"Excuse me," I say, taking Austria by the arm and escorting her inside, ignoring the *What Have I Done* chorus in my mind.

"Have a seat," I say, this time with only the slightest pretense toward courtesy, my lady tucked safely away in our room upstairs.

We sit quietly at the patio table, braving the treacherous waters of an uneasy calm. Nervous tranquility. Both of us craving to speak. Afraid to speak.

"What are you doing here?"

She looks at me with those witch eyes. A sorceress' eyes, head cocked slightly at my audacity. A breeze ruffles my shoulder length hair, which I intend to see down to my waist before I die.

"My daughter's done quite well for herself, I see."

She locks a gaze onto my bosom, unhidden in the tight, midnight blue summer pullover, cleavage on display at the top. In the war between the Sapphos, in the battle between her face and my breasts, I am victorious. Whether she is gripped by lust or laughter, I do not know. But I stiffen my posture nonetheless, drawing on the strength of my own upbringing, days and nights bound and whipped in the horse barn, being anally raped by my mother from behind on all fours in that self-same barn, with the twitching and low whinnying horses nearby.

"I can't believe you're here Mrs. Goldman. Hasn't Austria suffered enough?"

"Who's suffered enough, Mrs. Bishop? *'Austria'*, you call her? You? Me? Suffering goes both ways, Honey. Or maybe you're out of touch with that. Here in your... crystal palace."

"Everything I have, I earned. I worked just as hard as my billionaire husband did. Keeping this giant house cleaned and decorated and raising his five kids."

"Did you ever have to spank those kids?"

I have to clam up, take a deep breath and sit back in my chair, forgetting the sheer size of what lies just below my face, but reminded again from the beautiful woman's lustful stare.

"I've never seen breasts that big," she says. "On a woman your size."

"They're not to everyone's liking. But they are mine."

"You want to hear the truth? I've imagined myself having breasts like that. You're a lucky woman."

"So your daughter tells me. And speaking of your daughter, Ms. Goldman, what is it that you hope to accomplish by coming here now? After all these years apart? After the... after the life you two had together?"

"What do you know about the life we had together? Did you run off with a man and get pregnant at 17? Did you get cut off by your rich daddy because of it? Did you have to deal with people spray painting the 'n' word on your car in the parking lot of your job because your husband happened to be black? Did you have to bury that husband because he was killed by his mistress at age twenty two, when his little girl was only four years old? Did you have to work your ass off just so you could afford a decent roof over your head and food in your kitchen? Did you have to raise a smart mouth little crying yellow faced bitch that everybody knew was black even though you were white and didn't have a husband?"

"Why didn't you just move? Why didn't you find a place with people who were more accepting and more tolerant of mixed families? People who weren't so closed minded and small?"

"I tried. I tried to find the courage and the strength to just pack up and leave but where was I going to go? A single woman with a daughter, who every single man I ever met looked at and lusted after as though I were a whore for sale. I had a good job at a factory and I wasn't about to give it up. And I liked my house and I liked my neighborhood—"

"Why did you abuse your daughter?"

The question stops us both in our tracks, to listen for the answers in the breeze.

"Why did you abuse *yours*?"

"I never said I abused my—"

"You never said you didn't, Mrs. Bishop. In fact, you didn't have to say anything."

Hypocrisy is power. Ultimate shelter in the storm.

"Answer the question," I say.

"What I did... I did in the name of discipline. I spanked and whipped the skin off her because she *needed* it."

"Did she need to be raped?"

She pauses, as appalled as any parent accused of such is required to appear.

"I don't know what it is she told you... but I never raped her."

"Do you expect me to believe that?"

"Frankly, I don't care what you believe. And I'm only sitting here, listening to your lies because I came to see my daughter."

"You came to see your daughter get published and get paid."

"And so what if I did? I raised her, despite what you *think* happened between us. Would I like to share some of my daughter's wealth? Yes I would. She hasn't even been published yet and she's already famous."

"And you're worried. No, it's not money you want, is it? Its answers. You want to know what's in that book, don't you?"

The first crack in her façade appears, writhing her in a discomfort that only adds to her extraordinary appearance.

"Why... I could care less what's in the book. I only care about..."

"What she said about you. About what you did to her."

She sits back in her chair. Expression in control again—with eyes burning me through.

"I told you. I only care about Lee. And if you don't mind... I would like to see her. Or are you going to stand between a mother and her daughter?"

"Somebody should have stood between the two of you when she was born."

I think maybe, I finally land a blow of some power, which makes her lower her head in what looks like a flash of shame. For a second or two, she actually looks vulnerable.

"May I call you Sarah?"

"Please."

"Sarah… do you understand lust?"

"I think we all do, don't we?"

"I'm not talking about anything as trivial and mundane as a man's cock. I mean… something so deep, so strong inside your body that it comes out in your dreams. I can look at your body—and your eyes—and I know you understand. The need to just… to just lock yourself in a room and put your own nipples in your mouth until your body shakes."

Such a deep and abiding confession comes with an effort unimaginable, I know. Such a deep revelation about one's self does not come without a price.

"We all suffer the same human desires," I say. "On some level, I do understand that.'

"A lust that burns inside like a raging inferno. To where you sit in church sometimes trying not to think about wrestling the preacher's wife to the floor and tearing her blouse off and biting her tits hard enough to make her scream the name of God and Christ. To sit there in church every Sunday because you're afraid *not* to go, because you're afraid you'll die in your sleep and wake up in Hell. To sit there and have to push fantasies out of your brain? Begging God to help you not imagining yourself naked in the big, empty church wearing a realistic cock, holding a big wooden paddle, and beating the Hell out of the visiting Lady preacher's big, white ass until you see blood on the paddle? Lust that makes you imagine yourself sodomizing the same preacher woman and gagging her with a pair of her own stockings, pulling back on those stockings like a horse bridle, hard enough to hurt her neck while you try to literally fuck the *shit* out of her? Like I said before, Sarah, do you understand lust?"

In grieving, I have to close my eyes and allow the image of my youngest daughter's breasts in so-called punishment to wash through.

"Yes. I understand lust."

"Do you understand how it takes over your body? How it causes you to go too far? How it makes you do things you had never imagined were possible? How it takes control when you get angry, when you have to discipline your daughter for her smart mouth, for her insolent attitude, for her lying tongue? Have you ever pulled your daughter's hair, or pulled her by the ear to make her move quicker, and felt what the sound of her little voice does to you on the inside? The craving? The wildfire? The aching to dominate, to control, to break her mouthy little ass down to nothing? The itching between your legs that can't be stopped until you see blood?"

"You're talking about child abuse, Mrs. Goldman."

"I'm talking about *lust,* Sarah. And by the way, my name is Laura."

"I understand those feelings, Laura. But they still don't justify—"

"What do you know about feelings, Sarah? How can you feel anything here? In this Paradise? When's the last time you felt hunger? Exhaustion? Loneliness? Pain? Poverty? Deprivation? The need to have things you know you'll never be able to afford to buy? When has 'feeling' inside you been pushed and driven by the frustration of life? The pain of living?"

"Heaven on Earth is still Hell, Honey. And I wrote the *book* on loneliness. And yes, I know and cherish the location of my last sunset. My special carrying case—where I keep my pills and a bottle of wine. I know your lust, Laura. And I know your pain."

"Then you know that if I'm to live—if I'm to release this torture in my body, I have to see my daughter. I have to tell her that I swear to God and

Jesus that I never wanted to hurt her. I need to tell her that it came from what my mother did to me. I need to tell her that I remember being in the bathtub with my mother when I was five years old."

The beautiful woman's face loses every brick of stable beauty, and crumbles to brief ugliness, an expression unstable with the burden of sorrow, arisen as a ghost from the Heart of Memory. And though I do not want to, my vision hazes anyway, and I blink once to clear it through an irritated calm, and brave the tickle of both tears down my face.

"You were five."

"I was five. I was seven. I was nine. I was eleven. I was thirteen. She called it our 'Secret Game'. An enema tube right out of Sybil. Tucked between her legs like a penis. Slid up my backside. I swear to God I didn't understand. I swear to God I didn't."

The sobs coming from a woman this strong and beautiful have a power I can no longer deny. Involuntary effort lifts me to my feet, by natural human compassion, and I go over to the beautiful woman and stand in front of her, while she wraps her strong arms around me and cries hard into my bosom.

The beautiful woman at my breasts permeates my memory still. The look of her beautiful eyes closed in weeping, the way my skin had vibrated from her voice, the selfsame tingling that I had felt at times from her own daughter, who had cried there herself once, in the pain of some phantom recollection—the sorrow of the ages spilled over in mourning. But in the woman's daughter, there was a vulnerability I could not resist without exploiting; turning her sorrow, her want and need for emotional relief into an opportunity to satisfy my own sickness, and I had encouraged her to finish her grieving at the front of my exposed breast, licked and pulled upon long and hard, until my filthy self was doubled over in the standing position, enduring the waves of ecstasy that lit up and passed through.

Yes. I am a breast queen. Charged with carrying the heavy weight and burden of their sheer size, along with an unfathomable desire of fetish I had never understood before, even when I had punished Penelope by sucking her nipples to red and raw and pin cushion prickling. What punishments had she ever deserved? What infractions had ever served to warrant such fervent, disturbed secrets unperturbed, unabashedly unfurled by me? The fetish which I am, the sick and twisted person I have become escorts the beautiful woman upstairs, past the Woman of Antiquity on the wall, up to the Great Woman of Perpetuity in the portrait at the top of the stairs, gazing down at us both with an epic disdain, a judgment and knowledge undeterred.

What is it that I imagine might happen at the end of our little walk, in the bedchamber of lost souls? Where goest thine reconciliation, Dear Woman, Dear Mother of Straw? As we walk the upper Hall of Dreams, what spirits of wanton need flow my disquieted learning, my newfound yearning inside—the burning I have only yet to understand? How will I reintroduce you to the girl you have destroyed from birth, to the girl you raised in the Ghoul of Graveyard Gesture, whose body you pestered, whose spirit hath festered to oblivion because of thee? What is it that I imagine—Juna, Woman of Beauty—that may occur in the hours that remain, to reintroduce and reconcile Eve to her lonely serpent again? Why does my mind rest me upon my back, watching the two of you embraced, standing beside the bed in the deepest kiss possible, doing the fellatio of the tongue forbidden! Why is it of such felicitous never mind, that I am fed the image of myself upon my back, with one of my breasts held and nursed by the daughter, and the other breast by you, Woman—the other by the Beautiful Woman! Why does my groin ache with this unwelcomed, unwanted, unwished for fantasy, as I walk with you down the Hall of Grieving? *It's going to be all right,* I allow my lying, lascivious lips to lend, even while I imagine myself with your perfect melody in one hand, played in the key of C Major, with your daughter's song pitched in D minor in my other hand, my lips and tongue flashing and pulling back and forth between you both in groaning, grunting madness.

The bottom half of me aches this end of the world desire, as I escort this tall, strong and beautiful woman through the doors of sin, into the cauldron refuge of the upper room.

o, Austria my love! There is no reconciliation in the evening day! There is no epic rising, no mountainous manifestation of merriment and mirth! No, Austria my love—Forgiveness and Redemption hath not drawn nigh to thee! The serpent hath not transformed into the Dove of Peace—there is no love and harmony! Despite this grand and epic walk taken by the two of you in the evening, as I stand helplessly at the Window of Hope, watching it fade ever so slowly away, as the skies over New Bethlehem are bathed in amber, from the light of a dying sun! Despite the spirit of renewal I feel between you, the Spirit of Compassion, that of empathy and lost love restored!

What is this dish, Dear Austria, that tastes of this cold and bloody feast? Why hath Fate hidden the truth from us, so that our Destiny can be revealed? What otherworldly power must be, to convince you that this she-demon is turned into an angel of light that warms you over like a cold gourmet feast to be devoured—that melts your heart like a River of ice in the springtime—allowing you to flow into my room on the current of something called *magnanimous mollification*, or the release of a lifetime of suffering, flowing into my room where I have been buried alive in fear. You open my coffin lid in the deep twilight, dear Austria, to set my poor soul aflight! Only shame and strength conspires to keep my mouth closed when you come in the room, Dear Austria, having wanted to say *please don't leave me*, but being unable to carry on! Instead I close my mouth in epic waiting for the hammer on my head, to put me out of my misery for my premature burial. And when you look at me so casually in the early evening light, I watch you display the stupor of self-satisfaction; I watch you be drunk with the complacency so typical of humanity when its needs are met. And I watch your beautiful lips mouth the words in slow motion—*I'm going to forgive my mother*.

The words flow out of you as effortlessly as a wisp of warm mist on an ice cold day—vanishing in the air before me. And I have to endure the look in your eyes, my love; that sadistic gaze, the inner satisfaction you feel as you run the sword through, and watch me lower my head and grunt from the pain and sniff from the crying, as both my eyes overflow with tears unknown. Then I look up again, defeated as you take both my hands and say *look at me*—so you can look me in the eyes when I die. But no! There is no 'I will cherish these days we had for the rest of my life'—this torture you spare me, my love. Instead, you look me in the eye, and I watch your beautiful lips mouth another devastation in a slow motion breeze...*Will you marry me?*

To this, I can only look at thee without speech! Searching for either sincerity or the opposite, but finding only Love's Humility, and your own epic want and need! Upon this, I can only lean forward in my chair at our bedroom desk and fall upon thee, and sob and weep *Oh, God* upon thy spirit over and over again!

Oh yes, Dear Austria! I will forever love and marry Thee!

At my Austria's bidding, tonight I sleep alone. They are together in slumber now. In the darkest part of New Bethlehem, where the shadow of nighttime rests on them. Hours ago, I went to sleep in the heat of an arousal that climbed the slopes of Everest, imagining Austria had me pummeling this bitch to within an inch of her life and throwing her out onto the street just outside the gate. While I rested in the fetal position before I slept, my hand rested between my legs to pressing and a sneaky, secret rubbing too minor to achieve, which left me to drift off in something close to agony. But Irony's Will is absolute, paramount and profound, which imprisons me in a deep and dreamless coma, where awakening is impossible and highly unlikely. So how is it that I could have seen the beautiful woman emerge quietly from the hall, in the stealth of Amazonian Legend, creeping over to where I lay busty on my back?

From somewhere beyond sleep, I am suddenly aware of a great weight dropped on me, as if I lay under the felling of a Cherry Tree, whose branches have slammed pure fear down on top of me. I can feel the branches of the tree scratch my arms, as I struggle to breathe from the wind knocked out of me, unable to even conceive of being set free. But the tree vanishes quickly, and I swoon from the spirit world into this one, my eyes wide and gazing into the eyes of Thine, the Divine Eyes of her will and purpose unrefined...

I am held nearly immobile under the sheet, unable to free my arms to push and fight. In disbelief, I realize that no, I really *can't* breathe, and the silhouette that blocks my breath is a demon possessed woman who I thought I had met before, whose strength and power is nearly that which pertaineth to a man...

From underneath her hand over my nose and mouth, I can hear a pathetic and breathless whimper that I recognize as my own, a weak and helpless sound, lost in the noise of my own heartbeat, the burning in my lungs, and the sound of my own blood rushing through my ears...

And I suppose the deep and sudden calm I feel is the Calm of Death, a gift given to all prey at the very last, as I am overcome with a profound and inescapable return to sleep.

*G*od sure knows the number of moments that fly, the number of ticks on the clock flying by. At the end of this predetermination, after this brief moment in time, I awaken to a blurry sight in the early morning dark. A tallish, extremely shapely Woman of Beauty in the finest gray business skirt and snow white blouse, large diamond earrings and full makeup and ruby red lips, with yellow-blonded hair pulled back in characteristic fashion. And as my eyes begin to focus, as sanity tries to take hold, I feel two hard hits upon my lips (as sure as anything, they are *punches*), followed by hot iron pain in my head as my hair is pulled, and the pain burning my scalp pulls hard enough to evoke a quick, muffled yelp, while it pulls my tied up body from the bed and slams it to the floor. Yes. I guess that's why I cannot move. I am still in my white night gown, but tied like a rack of lamb by thin white ropes.

My shoulders ache in something like a cold throbbing, in contrast to the hot throbbing in my wrists bound behind my back. In the early morning dark, the ache in my body is transformed to fear, as the strong woman stands in fine clothes pulled from my dead daughter's closet, with black stiletto heels most certainly pulled from mine. I hear an angry, frustrated voice of helplessness scream the word *Momma* from somewhere near our space—amidst the words *please* and *don't do it*. Then the pain in my scalp returns, and drags me sliding like a sack of leaves across my bedroom carpet, then smooth and fast across the carpet in the hall, where I am powerless to stop the wall from slamming into me.

To whatever end would pointless screaming be, through the rag which muffles my mouth? Besides, Austria screams hard enough for the both of us, herself naked and bound tightly in the other room. The hands of time grip my hair hard and true, sliding me around and laid on my side in the lighted hall, so I am able to see the tragedy of my indecision in life. This stands before me an inch over six feet in high heels and red lips, as shapely hipped in a skirt as any woman I have seen on the white side of Jennifer Lopez and Kim Kardashian, but with the strong thighs and tight, small waist besides. The sight of this power, this Amazon perfection is my perfect humiliation, and I am suddenly ashamed of the fatness of my overdeveloped, watermelon sized tits. But these remain her desperation, I know, as she approaches me forthrightly and kneels down so prettily, and rips my gown open with a loud tearing of cloth, where my breasts both spill out so incredibly large to fathom.

My God, she says, her face briefly awestruck, her lips open in an amazement she cannot deny. She scans me while I lay on my side bound and gagged, two J cup breasts globed out in the cold open, outside of the torn white cloth, the front of them already drawn and erect in the early morning air. When I feel her hands take one as a great ball of dough, I can feel only fear and revulsion in their unwanted sensitivity, as she pulls the nipple and squeezes it so lovingly, burying her hands into the flesh, which makes me close my eyes in violation, resisting the breast rape, trying not to feel the unwanted pleasure that emanates through the fear in my body.

She gets down on her knees to get a better two handed feel, squeezing one breast with both hands, shaking her head once just so slightly, like a gold miner dying at the mouth of a mother lode. They are erogenous for so many women, but only to the slightest arousal, but where I can be brought to full steam and beyond by the long term squeezing of them alone. A blessing or a curse, I do not know, as she watches me squirm, trying to resist the feeling they bring to my groin.

And then we both hear *Mommaaaa!* Screamed so loud from the room down the Hall, which makes me stupidly turn my head towards the sound, to miss the contempt in Laura's eyes, the new frown on her beautiful features. I turn back to her, still gagged, making the dreaded eye contact, not wanting to read any message of doom in her eyes. And then, as the woman who must endure the Penetration of Lore, who must hearken the death of a part of who she is from this stabbing, this beautiful woman lowers her tightly bunned, blonde head, and in disbelief I must watch and feel without a blink, her pull my nipple far and complete into her mouth.

The whimpering *Oh God* is muffled in my throat, the blocked cry of prayer, rather than perversion this time. Her red lips are the Curse of Sin, to reminisce my mind of the blood I know is on my lips from her punches. The flesh of my breast is pulled upward like a great mountain peak pulled upward from the earth, but pulled by lips of ruby red, then let go in a loud, kissing sound. She does this again, to the erect nipple stained in lipstick, this time sucking once for the phantom milk that can never be, groaning a deep approval among a sigh just as wide and deep. It is the culmination of all forty nine years of her life, the un-hoped for dream of the impossible, even to what she dared not fantasize, while satisfying the years of ache upon her daughter's own breast and nipple.

This last pull, she savors. With wrinkled brow and anguished face. Eyes closed all the way up. Hearing the sound of my breathing mixed with her daughter's screams, finished by the kissing sound of my nipple being released from her lips once again.

*W*hen she opens her eyes and looks down, she sees the calm of uneasy acceptance; me in the aftermath of my own curse, though not to completion, but to where I could not have endured even a single moment further of what she has just done. While I stare at her eyes, my chest is alive by the rise and fall of breathing, the replenishing of energy for her, as a battery plugged in and charged for what must be. I hear the hopeless, failed and weakening cry from the other room, the doorway which lies beyond me down the hall. Her daughter's voice awakens her this time, and I see the same acceptance I feel fall over her. Then so mysteriously, so inexplicably, she steps into my room away from me for a time. Then she returns with a haughty leather purse of mine, black and classy, big enough to hold whatever tools a woman needs to get by. She places my own bag down on the floor in front of me, then reaches inside and pulls the long, black leather belt from within.

It may as well be a lady district attorney, or congresswoman or female professor I see knelt down before me. So well dressed. So composed. So compelling. So sophisticated in manner or appearance. This forty nine year old woman of seasoned beauty stands up with the belt and folds it, then walks calmly in black heels and stockings towards the other room, where I have heard the sound of the betrayed in mourning. Upon the well dressed woman's entrance, there is already the sobs more quiet, the disquiet of a grown woman who knows she is about to be whipped with a belt.

After the rising of a woman's voice in pleading, I hear the whacking of hard belt leather on soft, ivory skin. Skin golden yellow with new bruises, eyes blackened already from the continued punching suffered when I was unconscious, jaw swollen from this self same punching, shoulders bleeding from the bites administered—freely given. I have to close my eyes in defeat, moaning to a God I never loved before, wishing that I could feel his protection now against the evil that we do. '*Lead us not into temptation,*' the prayer says for a reason—'*deliver us from evil.*' From the temptation of a practiced sexual sadist, to the evil she hath wrought—my spirit bears witness to the naked daughter with ankles and behind-the-back wrists tied only, laid on her side on Penelope's bed, the rope tied so surreptitiously from her neck to the center carving at the head of the bed, lest she fall off the bed and hang herself.

I am witness in spirit only, to the naked young beauty being whipped with a folded belt by the older, more beautiful woman. In the Hall, bound and gagged so tightly, I pray to a God who cannot hear me, as I listen to the daughter scream of what she didn't mean and of being sorry, and the deeper-voiced older woman screaming of 'books' and 'private business' and 'obeying' and 'since you left me' and 'caring about your soul' and 'slutting a fucking dyke' and 'I told you God would bring you back' and 'If thou beatest with a rod' and so on, all of this to the rhythm of leather snapping against naked skin, then a pause and a change in the snapping and the screams, sounds now tempered by the noise of a belt buckle tearing into skin, and the choking screams of a woman pulling against the rope tied around her neck.

The noises double my helplessness to a state of panic, and I struggle in one last strain and shake without moaning, turning over in time to my gigantic tits flopping from one side to the other.

*A*fter many untold minutes, she emerges in the aftermath of trauma; a stern, tired look on her still lovely mature features, never looking more like a mother than this moment, walking toward me without reservation, causing me to prepare for the sting of leather across my breasts which will surely reduce me to the tears in waiting. But she only walks past me—turning me over so I can see. She tosses the belt down, as if finally for the last time. If the belt were white, I would be able to see that it is stained with blood. But it lays there black, like the serpentine of old reborn, resting in the shadows of the forest trees—the trees of sentimental youth planted and grown. In the shadows of these selfsame trees, I lay too exhausted to move, weary of the faint nostril breathing, watching her move in the spirit of humility now. Able to accept that the beautiful woman is done with pretense, and must disrobe to her true self, to reveal the deeper parts of truth itself—this, the second part of the truth, which has her facing away from me, still in the stilettos, removing the blouse first to show me that what lies beneath is no illusion—the fit, strong middle aged body kept fit by 30 years of protein, factory labour, fasting and fanaticism.

She makes slow work of the skirt next, down and away from a tiny, athletic waist and hips set wider than most could believe—super-heroine wide and Lopez deep, they are. An Ass for the Ages, it is. Dropped and spread by what only Time could perfect, to a prime and fearsome dimension. Extraordinary, with too much substance to ignore, in teardrop and upside-down heart shaped perfection, but with power. And then the black bra is unlatched to reveal perfect breasts, breasts hung so delicately with time, softened to a mouthwatering jiggle by the years of womanhood. The stockings are next, which must bid adieu to the black shoes on their way out, rolling softly down and away—down long, white legs younger and smoother than their years, this done twice, still standing until both stockings are pulled ceremoniously away from her lovely feet. But this is not a fantasy for my twisted sleep. No. What I am witnessing is as real as my own condemned reflection in the mirror, staring alive and judging back at me before I went to bed.

Then at last, from over the bubble of her ass slides down the black, French cut underwear cloth, to reveal fully what I now understand is the origin of her daughter's, whose own bottom came not from the jungles of her Father's great ancestry, but from the small town suburbs of her Mother's pedestrian life. But it is the Momma version—so unbelievably the counter-part to my top half; a bottom that would have to be seen to be believed. In this unclothed vessel, a goddess kneels down and reaches into the bag for the second part of the Truth, which when she removes it, makes my eyes well up with tears, grunting '*no*' as clearly as I can through the cloth in my mouth. She squats facing me so that I may see what God has given her, then slides something up deep into herself—closing her eyes and holding her head back in requisite fashion, purely for my sake alone. Then she stands and gathers the straps of it tightly around those hips, until I can clearly see now the extremely realistic member hanging down, on the edge of true bigness, and myself now on the edge of true terror.

She tightens the harness straps, then takes hold of the member hanging down as though it were her own, rubbing it at least twice in a full stroking motion, her face in the frown of a knowledge so deep as to only be understood by her. *This is my cock,* my mind hears her spirit say, as she opens her eyes to look at me, unashamed. The tears are heavy on my face, seeming to weigh my head down to the floor in defeat, where I can only see the whitened feet of clay, which take the fateful steps past me, down the hall and into my daughter's old room, to where her daughter is in dread and waiting.

I am defeated. Resigned to helplessness. Resting wearily now, feeling the flow of tears tickle down past my nose and cheek laid against the floor, as I am turned slightly forward now upon my bosom. I barely have the strength to react, when I hear the daughter begin the hopeless wailing again, but this time in as sane a pleading as possible; declaring love for her mother, saying that *God loves you and he doesn't want you to do this,* which I know shudders the woman's angry resolve to a sad surrender—a giving in to what dark destiny must be. I am still but a witness only in spirit, as the mother forces the daughter onto her stomach, the rope still tied to the daughter's neck. On her daughters' back, undeterred by the wrists tied nearby, she puts no liquid, no lubrication of any kind on the big member, or in her grown daughter's bottom, relishing the breathless sobs, the hopeless crying, the hapless squeezing of the buttocks to try and prevent penetration. But in the strength of her calling, aided by the heat of sweat and fear, she pushes the big member slowly, painfully up her daughter's rectum, which I can hear and feel in the changing of the scream; from that of a frightened little girl in a woman's body, to the Womanhood of Eve and Understanding, and the burning of blue and black fire.

The Mother lays there full and heavy, the inch times eight slid up her daughter's bottom, to where the pain is that of ripping and tearing and splitting and burning. Austria's screaming is endless, as is the well of tears reopened, where there is a renewed and gushing flow of water and misery. For the better part of an hour, the cries ebb and flow among the quiet, as the woman squeezes with an agonizingly slow rhythm, waiting. Unafraid of the long and painful wait, and the culmination of this patience un-delayed—this perseverance un-denied. And when the better part of this hour has passed, she knows of the trouble she is in, the horror of what she must now endure, so sorry now that she allowed the spirits to take over the squeezing, seeing her own backside widened in her mind as if out of her own body and looking from above, wishing now to be filled from behind within herself, but to no avail.

Oh, Lord, let this cup pass from me, she says so loudly… *forgive my white nigger bitch for her sin—repent… repent you nigger bitch,* I hear her say, as if hearing a voice from the past. *You mix-blood cunt*, she says, in a voice so strangely possessed of deepness, as though channeling energy from beyond herself. And then I hear *Oh God and Holy Jesus, you fucking nigger bitch God and Holy Jesu*—the syllables upon which I hear the most inhuman sound I have imagined from a woman, a high pitched wailing howl as if a she-wolf were stabbed in the gullet. This sound continues on and on, until the unholy power passes through her body and into the mansion, flying the halls of early morning darkness, touching fear and cold to my skin.

*T*here were times when I felt unloved by everybody. My husband, my children, my mother, my sisters. Teachers…every so-called friend I've ever had. Across the barren landscape of my life, through the wandering wilderness of want for company and a connection with somebody, I had found someone to love, and someone to love me. And we shared a bond at once so much greater than love, but a deep and abiding loneliness, a sorrow given to us by the women who brought us into this evil world unwanted, and raised us unliked, and even to where we were unloved by them. And now, the only person who ever loved me lies bleeding in the room down the Hall, bound up like a hog to be struck down and slaughtered. These spirits of Disillusionment, Depression and Despair are a part of me, riding me like a saddle bred horse from here to a lonely grave.

Truly, the pain of the ages steps out of the room. Tallish and nude, spent, her member coated red in the aftermath of its calling. On my back, I'm able to see clearly now, watching her walk nude down the carpeted hall toward me, causing me to wonder if the blood of her instrument is about to be mixed with my own. But she steps so calmly past me, her white thighs stained with blood—and she releases the straps just enough, then slides the power point from inside her, then lets the whole of it fall down her legs like a pair of drawers to the floor.

My eyes are wet with the haze of memory. A weeping born from nowhere, to none effect, relieving none of the sorrow I feel. Doing nothing to assuage the fear. She stands for a moment, ignoring me, then kneeling down to her leather bag, my leather bag, reaching inside, removing a small, sharp blade the size of a kitchen paring knife, then she moves over to where I am and turns me over towards her, ignoring the muffled pleading and moaning.

I feel the blade suddenly at my face, cold and sharp, touching my skin so delicately. Having the power of a taser to spark trembling in my whole body. Then I feel pressure on the stocking so tightly bound, and movement of the knife against the pressure until the gag is cut, and the pressure relieved is so profound that I moan involuntarily, already pushing my white underwear cloth out of my mouth with my tongue. My jaws ache, the muscles are on fire when I try to move. *In the name of God*, I say, *have mercy*. But she looks at me in the tranquility of battle mode, and says *I'm going to stab you in the leg with this knife*. This brings the new flow of tears, the requisite shaking of my head, the characteristic pleading and begging for nonexistent compassion.

She rolls me close to her, enjoying the music of pleading, recharging from the sound of my voice, taking a good, strong hold of my tied up body. Even when I feel her suddenly tense up, I can hardly believe it's happening until I feel a stick of white orange heat burn through the muscle of my thigh and hear the loud, deep scream come on its own from deep inside. The walls echo with the sound of my scream. Then the echo is layered by another, as she works the knife back and forth enough to hear a human soul suffer an echo of Hell itself. Then I feel the heat dissolve as she stands up with the knife, watching me writhe and cry from the pain.

I play this agony as the keys of a violent sonata, bathing our arena with the sound of a woman's voice in great travail. I make the Heavens aware of me, uncompromising in my loss of dignity. I continue this until she kneels naked beside me again, touching her finger to the blood, telling me to open my mouth and stick out my tongue, which I am too afraid not to do. And yes, it is true, that blood is flavored with the taste of iron. She rubs a streak of blood on my face as well, then cleans the rest of the knife on my breasts roughly, as if she might decide to cut them at any moment. But even when a city is destroyed, often the great works of art are rescued for posterity. For history's sake, she leaves no further cut upon my skin, then returns to her bag one last time, placing the small knife and the bloody member inside.

And then I see the naked woman remove a longer carving blade. All of seven inches I can tell. She stands, holding the long knife, listening to my long and helpless sobbing again, my desperate calls for her humanity, and for her to have mercy on the both of us. And when she is fully charged again, she gathers her strength, taking each fateful step past me towards the other room, powered along by the very word I use, the word *no* in repetition, having profoundly the opposite effect on her. Yes, the Third Part of the Truth is lifted in cold steel, to exact punishment upon the living.

While my leg burns from the stabbing, while my gut aches from the sobbing, the witch takes every easy step toward the room, this part of the truth in sharpened blade, for what comeuppances that must be paid. Yes, we all have a dark destiny, which we will meet, except we be pulled miraculously from the Death Train. But upon this path, she strides in nudity, force and power. Turning the corner in beauty—holding firm the third part of the truth—which is cataclysm.

And to my gravest expectation, I must close my eyes in total defeat, pushing the last of the tears free when I hear the pitiful voice choke these same words *no* in repetition, then I hear her begin to call the name of our Lord and Savior, but to what end—for what purpose? Where is his blessed spirit, the only spirit of goodness to have ever walked the Earth? Where is his Holy presence, when she begins the loud and unmistakable siren of the Death Scream, the woman's scream that is powered as the castrati; with height and width, depth and volume, the three dimensional scream of revelation—the realization, the confrontation with the Spirit of Fear, born from the Spirit of Death.

She screams a crimson dying. The Bloody Murder of Legend, which torments the dreams and fears of every man, the low and highs of heightened flight of mind, where fear slides lightning through every frightened nerve and bone. I strain to hear the sound of the knife blade going in, but I cannot; I only hear the loudest possible scream, penetrating my ears and brain in pinpoint torture of blade, to cut me from the inside out by precision, while I listen to many untold minutes of death by the cold of hate and steel. And even in the midst of these death screams, I hear an animal declaration, the sound of demonic rage channeled through a woman, a sound even stronger than the fearful shrieks from the other.

I lay here. Bleeding. Crying. Dying both outside and in. Cursing the day I was born into a world capable of such—cursing the sound I hear now, which is the hard grunting of rage and effort, when the scream of fear has finally passed. The knife sound I had dreaded comes to me now, to inspire the Truth in the Theatre of My Mind, which shows me the naked, white skinned woman stabbing repeatedly the lifeless body of the yellow skinned woman lying bloody on the bed.

Of how many dozens of stab wounds I see, of how many dozens of them I feel, this I can hardly tell. Of the *one hundred and seventy two* stab wounds in my beloved's body, from these I can never tell.

hen, from Hell she emerges. Bloody from her face to her forearms, from her hands to her knees. Still holding the Sword of Truth dipped in blood, that carries a message of pure eschatology. In this cathedral, this Great House of Worship, this shrine to the pride of life— through the Hall of Prosperity, she walks free. Unburdened by the heavy calling that has pressed down on her since her daughter was a little girl, when she first pinched her in church to make her stop kicking her feet and humming to herself; since that day after church, when she could not resist what came next, to see the fear on her little daughter's face on the drive home.

I'm going to spank the skin from your backside when we get home, she said.

Hmm? What did you say? Her daughter had said. *What did you say Momma—*

Shut up! She had barked like a big beautiful dog. A quick and powerful voice—to send her little girl's finger straight to her own lips, her little forefinger nail to her little teeth in a nervousness unknown—the nervousness that leads to fear.

Laura walks toward me. Unburdened now, free from the Call of the Executioner. Yes, that proverbial Executioner's Song so well known. Free from the heavy weight of Eve. The curse from the Garden of Antiquity. I watch the Angel of Death passing by. Strolling to where the leather bag of punishment was wrought. Kneeling down. Placing the blood stained blade inside and far away from view. And when her hand emerges again, I now understand the Greatest Fear of Man. The Unknown Terror. The one that lies beyond the Fear of Death.

It is the Fear of Hell.

The fear of an eternity away from God, which grips my immortal soul where there is no calm, but only the fearful expectation of Divine Retribution, for a life lived in rejection of the Truth. But there is a barrier raised. An obstruction between me and the Divine now—a barrier that falls away with the solid ground, to reveal a great Gulf affixed, betwixt me and my so-called Paradise beyond. In this terror, this fear which paralyzes the body, I watch her stand naked and bloody over me, her womanhood visible, split by nature, mocking me to scorn.

She squats and straddles my roped body, with me on my back bound, and looking down the so-called barrel—of what comes next along the timeline. Were I not paralyzed with fear, I would writhe and scream. But to move, or make a sound? I cannot. Then she lifts the rod of iron away from my face, then pushes my breasts up and together, holding them there with one hand. Then with the other hand, she puts the barrel of the pistol deep inside her mouth, and I hear a sound like a quick and loud, explosive *pop*—that splatters blood from nowhere onto the opposite wall.

The sound I hear now is a woman screaming. But from whenceforth cometh this fervent scream? My mouth is open, my breath comes and goes in time to this noise—so yes, yes it is me. With the beautiful woman laid folded back on top of me, I remember the shock in her eyes when she pulled the trigger, and the way her straddled legs had betrayed her dying brain and stayed where they were, and her naked body had folded backward on her legs, straddling me in death, oppressing me inside what little life it is I have left. Underneath the dead woman laid back on me.

I scream relentlessly. Unrelenting. Unrepenting the loss of dignity, or my sudden loss of a need for the Gates of Paradise.

The last days of New Bethlehem loom above me in gray and weeping, in rolling thunder and lightning from the clouds, swirling through the cemetery forest trees with purpose and warning. These summer rains do fall in grieving. In sorrow for what the clouds have seen, for the revelation of the inner heart of man and woman, and for the judgment of souls that must be. And though I sit in so-called safety, sheltered in

Cadillac Luxury from the rain, my heart is as heavy as these summer storm clouds, and when I close my eyes, the waters of my memory still flow. I don't know if there is a space under Heaven where I can go, a place under the stars where I can hide from the memory of Laura Goldman. Nor from the love I had for her daughter.

It is written, that Fate decides over reason, that Destiny overrides indecision. Despite the public and private outcry, the publication of Austria's book, of Austria's life has been put on hold indefinitely. As to the pages of that serpent I read, I do not know whether or not it would sail the waters of glory, or sink in humiliation to the bottom of the sea. Perhaps someday, when the wound has healed, and the tragedy of our lives has come and gone. Do these same clouds weep over the grave of Austria's mother, buried a thousand and twenty five miles down east, interred beside a loving husband lost a quarter century before she died? Do these clouds send Waters of Renewal for her spirit that roams free, the ghost that walks the land of blood and rain, grieving to be set free?

Laura! Thou wicked and perverse generation! How can you escape eternal damnation! Even while the memory of her burns my body, to torment my mind in Hellish sleep, I know that somehow, some way, the God of History was able to reach down from infinity, and cleanse the evil from her immortal soul, though her body was racked by the curse of sin unto death. Then upon this realization of that eternal love, that despite her hell bound condition, that her body lies accursed in the grave, apart from a soul washed as white as snow, I am burdened under these weeping clouds with the Sorrow of the Ages, which tears into my flesh to make me tremble, and from the pit of my stomach emanates a long and continuous wailing, that swirls in the air around me like a spirit, to take form as the words *I'm sorry* over and over again, until the image of the Cross bears down upon my soul, and I must cry yes, and bow down in my heart to Him. I'm struck suddenly by the power of what almost was, of how close I had come to the fiery pit, and an eternity away from the Light. My soul is now heavy laden with gladness, a relief so epic as to be unendurable, which burdens me down with sobs and weeping. But when this weeping is done, I know that the spirits that haunt me are not done, and that whether or not I shall see Paradise, the curse of this life may be a weight too profound, and a burden too solemn and heavy to bear.

Wishing to be rid of the grave, and the spirits that live here, I take my umbrella up, as black as my shoulder length hair has always been, opening the car door into the storm, not caring at all whether the lightning will find me at my lover's grave. Through the grieving rain I stroll, leg burning with what has happened, causing me to walk very slowly, disguising the limp that begs to be seen. Slowly I drift beneath the black umbrella—long, black summer wind coat in place, red rose in hand, braving the winds of warning that blow. Austria Lee Goldman is the name that is above every name in my life, moving towards me on the gravestone, above the mound of a freshly laid carpet of flowers and green grass sod.

I arrive at the grave and sinister sight, unable to draw comfort from it at all. *But I love her, and I love her,* sings the cello whine above that in pizzicato, as I place the bright red flower atop the grave in proper pose. In requisite repose, there is the prose and poetry of action, the ceremony of women and men, to draw hope and meaning from where there is none. The happy wedding days and white rose flowers that presage unhappiness and divorce so often—the happy graduations in pomp and circumstance, transformed into a funeral march of the deluded, and a life of epic financial struggle and failure. The prayers and bouquets and tears shed for the bodies beneath the earth; verses of God's mercy read over the souls of the damned. But in quiet, without the clamour of human voice and guile, I place this rose in the name of God, thanking him for what brief flash of mercy there has been.

And when the name *Austria* passes through my spirit, there is a determined gust of wind, blowing the rose free from the gravestone, pulling my umbrella hard, the way it has threatened to since I got out of the car, finally inverting it in classic style—with rain pelting my eyes closed, until I have to let the umbrella go, and watch it be taken too fast for me to run after it with this sore leg. I am amazed to see it go, reshaped to its former self, taken as if by spirits that float and run towards the distant bottom of the hill. And then the wind picks up again, bending the tree above me in noisy surrender, whishing a message of latter day warning, and of what must befall the end of the age we are in.

Looking down at my feet, there is the red rose I placed, blown steady against my shoe. I reach down to pick it up, knowing that it is mine again.

The End

*T*his is a lawn of devastating beauty. The grieving shores of eternal life, or eternal damnation. Walking through the booming, crackling storm, I know that I must return to the Cherry Orchard, to gather my affairs in their proper order, to decide what corner of this Earth where I must flee. Whether or not there will be my beloved pills and a glass of wine, I do not know. Curses be to the rod of iron, the pistol which haunts my dreams, or to the airplane flight above the tropical western island shore, where the door is unlocked and flung open in the wind by me, where I am sucked and carried into the clouds. In the wet, weeping world, of these things, I cannot know. Of my beloved pills and a glass of wine... I can never know.

S. B.

Jonathan Lovejoy

ABOUT THE AUTHOR

Jonathan Lovejoy is a graduate of the University of North Carolina at Greensboro, with a B.A. in Religious Studies, and a graduate of Liberty University with an M.A. in Theological Studies. He currently lives in Winston Salem, North Carolina.

For more info on the author's life and career, visit jonathanlovejoy.com.

www.ingramcontent.com/pod-product-compliance
Lightning Source LLC
Chambersburg PA
CBHW071307170626
46809CB00001B/354